Girl Get the Wine

by Em Rina and A.M. Lee

Table of Contents

Wine Pairings

Red - Serious, heartfelt, with a hint of drama
My First Heartbreak
Seabass
Business or Pleasure?
The Fire Exit
Networking

White - Easy, chilled, with a flare of spirit
The Lock
They Ran out of Asparagus
A Thousand Years Later
Number 74
His Latest Heartbreak

Champagne & Rose - Charming and delicate
My First Heartbreak
Spices and Bubbles
Jack
You Are Not A Bag Of Chips

Other - When wine isn't strong enough...
Old Photos
The Letter

Rules Learned from Dating in London

1. If he says he likes the tube - he is just trying to come home with you
2. Date your neighbours with caution [you will have to see them on your street again]
3. If you can't decide, let the wine decide
4. He did not get finger surgery and his phone is not broken
5. If his stuff is gone - no, you haven't been robbed, you have been left
6. I can't address this enough; always have an emergency bottle of wine
7. Woman up and just make the first move
8. You are not a circus employee, do not entertain the clowns
9. Bubbles with a spicy food is never a good idea
10. Never think "Nothing can get worse"
11. Always double check the bathroom lock when you are on a date
12. There is such a thing as "too much of a gentleman"
13. Men do gossip…
14. It is only acceptable to be a ghost during a Halloween party
15. Food poisoning on Saturday morning is not actually food poisoning
17. Unless they work shifts, if they initiate texting after 22:30 five times within the first four weeks, then they're a clown.
18. Make sure you know if its a date, hangout, or work event so you can dress accordingly
19. Do not cry over someone who doesn't know the difference between 'your' and 'you're'
20. If you think "Ah it is not like I will see him again!".... you probably will
21. Sometimes you do not get the closure or apology you wanted

F*ck No Clown List

If you find yourself on this list it is because you have been found to have displayed clown behaviour. As a result, you are a clown. Any persons being found to text anyone on the FNC list will be punished by paying for all drinks at the weekly Wednesday Night Dinner.

1. Clowtin - Riley

Reason: After second unsuccessful date, Clowntin came to my street at 03:00 screaming my name

2. Arthur - Em

Reason: He insisted on paying for our food, but once there wasn't a second date he emailed me an invoice for the food when he had _insisted_ on paying

3. The King of the FNC (aka the Lord)- Em

Reason: Full of himself

4. CanISpeakToTheManagerClown - Chanel

Reason: Complained over a soap in a hotel and asked for a refund

5. Barista dude - Chanel

Reason: Spoke for a full hour about how he used to make coffee for an A -List movie star but refused to tell who it was but kept going on and on and on about it. Then got upset at the fact Chanel owned a cafe

6. TheOneWithSmallDickEnergySyndrome (Mr. SDES) - Riley

Reason: Told me that in order for me to date him I should change my career as "female's shouldn't be lawyers"

7. Michelle - Jess

Reason: Spoke about her ex during most of the date

8. Chicken farmer - Chanel

Reason: Said he had a few chickens in his tiny London flat. Had not one, not two, but seven chickens

9. James M - Jess

Reason: Introduced his parents over a facetime on a first date, even though I asked him not to

10. AC (The one with arm chair) - Riley

Reason: He rocked up to our date with an armchair, like it was totally normal

Introduction

I've been happily single for about five and a half years. Okay, I know what you're thinking...happily single? Yes. Five years and three months of glorious, albeit sometimes exhausting, adventures in the world of London dating. Besides the normal moments of butterflies in my stomach, sadness from disappointment, and embarrassing moments where you just want the world to swallow you whole there have been moments that deserve to be immortalised. Maybe not the guys...but the moments definitely.

The moments when his dad was the chauffeur, when I cried because he only left me a can of tuna, when the fire exit was the quickest way out, or when I tripped over flat pavement while racing down the street of Central London in heels at twilight. Yes, I've met some interesting characters but the moments that have starred them are the stories that have kept me and my friends in stitches.

What can I say? My life was meant to be a book.

So when I say that I am happy, I truly mean I am happy. Dating just to date is fun. Someone might say my London dating life has been pretty chaotic.

Chaotic but entertaining.

***

***

Before I tell you about my present, you have to understand my past.

***

\

I
My First Heartbreak

Wine Pairing: Champagne with Lemonade

***

My first heartbreak was at eighteen. Are you really surprised? Everyone's first heartbreak was around eighteen.

The story is always the same. You thought that he was the one. The one you were going to end up with. The one that would father your children, who would go to the same schools you did. You fell in love with them in year four and finally got together in year nine and stayed together through exams, only to be dumped the week after.

As you can probably imagine, the pain of that heartbreak was like nothing I had ever felt before. I was in bed for weeks, sleeping in his old hoodie, amongst the empty chocolate wrappers that were strewn across my bed. We might look back at our young heartbroken selves now and laugh but I don't think we truly remember how horrible it felt in the moment. Those moments are the ones that set the foundation for the way that we deal with every heartbreak and disappointment that follows for the rest of our lives.

Uni wasn't going to start until September. My childhood best friend Maddie and I had promised ourselves that after our exams, we would take a post-exam holiday. I wasn't about to let a stupid boy ruin what was supposed to be the best summer of my life. So, in addition to his hoodie that I would sleep in, I grabbed my tiniest bikinis, shortest summer dresses, and most comfortable heels, threw them into my carryon and headed for Rhodes.

For this trip, we had gone all out. We had decided to spoil ourselves and get the sea view room with the money we had saved by not getting air-con. This backfired. The room was small and hot. There was a view, if you count the reflection of the sea from the building across the way. But, we were two young Finnish girls on their first grown up holiday. We were more concerned about having enough cider, Smirnoff, and Breezers in the fridge, and enough lemon juice to highlight our already blonde hair.

The first night, we got dressed up and went out for dinner at the restaurant in the hotel to toast our success. Like the classy ladies we were, we drank an entire bottle of champagne, mixed with lemonade, to complement our luxurious salad dinners. Surprisingly, we didn't leave the hotel that night as we drank and danced the night away at the hotel bar. We woke up in our sweatbox room still wearing yesterday's makeup with a headache and the taste of cheap champagne stale in our mouths. The rest of the day we ate like hippos by the pool and chatted about how a heartbreak was the most effective diet and how we should get our hearts broken more often. Did we mean this? No, but I needed to distract myself from the hurt somehow, so what better way than to laugh at myself?

Needless to say, the next four days followed a similar pattern. We woke up around twelve and went down for breakfast around two, only to be told that we had missed it again, so had to suffice with a tube of Pringles each, as we needed something in our stomach to be able to drink the hydrating coffee. Then we would attempt to sit by the pool for a few hours while suffering the "worst hangover of our lives" before inevitably returning to the room to cry and deposit the contents of our stomach into the toilet while the sun beamed through the open window. There we would wait for life to return to our dehydrated souls. At least we had the view.

On the fifth night, our wallets couldn't handle another night out, so we spent the day by the seaside tanning and the night watching Spanish telenovelas while nursing our last remaining ciders. Back at home, we had booked tickets to a water park for the next day. Foreshadowing the mature adults we would become, we thought that showing up hungover would not be the best idea.

However, in the morning I woke up with what felt like third degree burns on my stomach and neck. I was as red as a chili pepper and felt about as hot as one. My tiny bikinis would not work today, so I figured I would pick up a one-piece on the way to the park.

Much to the surprise of the front desk, we made it to breakfast that morning. True to form, we ate about three days' worth of breakfast in one sitting which was probably a surprise to the chefs who must have been used to getting at least some of the breakfast back on a daily basis.

While waiting for the 11:30 bus, we stopped in a corner shop to look at their swimsuits. I didn't like any of the options so we decided to look at a shop closer to the water park, figuring there had to be something cute there. After all, I was single. The new love of my life might be at the park.

The bus ride was beautiful. If there is one thing that Rhodes is, it is beautiful. The clear water gleaming brightly in the sun brought about a promise of a stress-free, hangover-free, heartbreak- free fun day. The two of us, fresh from exams (and boys) enjoying the sun in a water park. I hadn't even cried in 48 hours. Nothing could go wrong today.

We got off the bus to find there were no local corner shops, and so I was forced to buy a new swimsuit from the water park store. I mean the colour was kinda cute; if you liked mustard yellow with "Fun in the Sun - Rhodes Water Park" in bright pink covering a map of the park. At least we wouldn't get lost.

Looking ridiculous is my forté. Having been tall all my life, I was used to wearing something that either wasn't in style or didn't fit right so I embraced the aesthetic and went like a freshly printed billboard to grab a floaty to go down the biggest waterslide in the park. The attendants looked us up and down as they handed us disgustingly purple inflatable tubes and laughed behind us as we ran off like the excited children we were.

We went down slide after slide and then floated down endless miles of currents that blessed our tired bodies and souls. When we were hungry, we grabbed our purple tubes and made our way to the food area, laughing at our stupid antics and jokes like when I dared Maddie to go hug the cute lifeguard. As revenge, she went to an information point and asked them to make an announcement for my "birthday". We also tried to photobomb as many couples as we could.

We were young. We had no immediate responsibilities. We were laughing at our freedom. After the previous tumultuous months, this was the first time I'd felt truly alive in weeks.

Then, he was right in front of me.

No. Literally.

He was standing right in front of me. In this water park. In Rhodes.

With another girl.

She was immaculate. Dark eyes, darker hair, and unburned skin. Her bikini complimented her perfect skin and dark complexion in a way that only someone with true fashion taste could pull off. Her hair was wet yet still made her look beautiful. She wasn't wearing any makeup, but she didn't need it. She could have been a *Sports Illustrated* model.

He turned around.

Damn it.

"Hi Em," he said in shock. "What a coincidence." He paused, searching for the right thing to say. "Well…have a good time." He walked away.

I couldn't breathe. I was still standing there, looking like a cheap cut out from the amusement park that had been stolen and tossed into the endless river.

She turned and did a quick double take on my swimsuit. She gave me a look of sympathy and a small, sweet smile as she ran to catch up with him, unknowingly clasping the hand that had once been mine to hold.

Screw my life. She was just as lovely as she looked.

"Well, it can't get worse than that."

Turned out…it could.

Rhodes is a small island. We saw them three more times.

Once at a restaurant, where I had to sit and watch him give her the rose he never gave me.

The second time, well technically I didn't see them…or I don't remember seeing them. But I was told the next morning that I'd acted completely composed before throwing up in a bush outside our hotel. I'm not sure which part they saw.

The third time I held myself with complete dignity as they stood in the queue far ahead of us while we waited for our lunch, hiding behind a particularly large group of people.

Six missed breakfasts. Twenty-five empty bottles. Twelve empty Pringles cans. One bad sunburn. One ex-boyfriend. One new girlfriend. Zero one-night stands. Four drunken make-out sessions (two each - hey, we needed all the wins we could get). The holiday we planned? No, but at least we didn't get herpes.

***

***

So how did I end up in London?

Paris is the city of lovers. New York is known as the city of opportunity. So why did I pick London? Because London is fun. It's the perfect place for people who want to explore and learn about themselves. There are art museums for self-discovery, parks for solo picnic dates, rooftop bars for nights with the girls, and buildings so majestic that you get lost in their history.

I had several options for university in Finland but I wanted to live life on my terms. So on a whim, I decided to apply to a university in London to study marketing. By some chance I got in and I have lived here ever since. Over the last seven years I've met a lot of people but the ones that have enriched my life tenfold are my friends. My trio of cheerleaders. My support system. My London family. My girls.

First there is Chanel. Chanel is the type of person that has inspired millennia of artists to paint but who have never quite captured their sitters true beauty. No matter how much you try, no one can turn away from her. At least, I couldn't when I randomly bumped into her on the stairs at work years ago. She was the most beautiful person I had ever seen which I'm pretty sure were my first words to her. She thought I was weird, but I somehow convinced her to be my friend. Since leaving that job she has opened up her first cafe in South Bank which has become our emergency headquarters.

Then we have Jess. Like myself, Jess is also an expat-except she isn't from Finland. She's from California. Based on my own Google searches one drunken girl's night, her parents are well-respected leaders in the Asian American Actors Association and they are well known in the industry. However, she firmly states that she doesn't know everyone in Hollywood. She left years ago so she could teach in London, but we like to tease her about it anyway on movie nights or when we see a fit actor. All jokes aside, Jess is the kind of friend that every girl should have. She is strong, supportive, and the one to hold you when you have to hear the harsh truth from Riley.

Riley: the giver of hard truths, fiercest of friends, and loyalist of supporters. Riley. The one who has been by my side the longest. We met in New Zealand on a holiday trip a few years ago. She came up to me in our hostel bar and pointed out that my shirt was a bit see through. I thought she was being a bitch but then she offered me her jacket to cover it up as the guys near her were making rude comments. Since that moment we have been fast friends. We quickly discovered that we were both in London and decided to live together even though we had only known each other for 20 minutes. We did eventually, for a bit, until I moved in with a boy.

**

***

I had been dating for fun, but I never truly fell in love…

…Until Rex

***

II
The One Who Flew Away

Wine Pairing: La Grupa Malbec Syrah 2018 x2

***

"Just pretend for a moment that you're walking down the street, enjoying the sun turning to twilight as the summer evening begins. The world is coming alive, with people just starting to relax after a long week at work. I'm on my third whisky on the rocks when you walk by. You're a vision floating on air. I stare as you walk past. You do a double take. You smile. My heart flips but you keep walking. If this was a movie, I would have found you the next day in the elevator, we'd get married, and we would tell our kids about the time we locked eyes and just knew."

The start to the perfect love story. At least, that's how he used to say it.

++

I've locked eyes with many boys. But very few have made me do a double take, and even fewer have made me understand how Taylor knew he was trouble. He didn't walk in, but I walked by, and that was enough to know that there would be a story written about us.

It wasn't until a few months later that we would meet; he would tell me his tale and I would remember mine.

How often do you walk past someone twice in a lifetime? How many times do you remember walking past them months later? Especially in a city as populous and diverse as London. Except, we did.

Months later, we locked eyes again. The girls and I were sitting at our seats at the Backyard Cinema when he walked past with his boys. This time, he mustered up the courage to come and talk to me. The chill of the first properly cold autumn night was setting in outside. Inside the secret movie theatre and past the hidden doors the show was about to begin. The flowers draped across the screen, the fog machine blew magic around the room, and the flutes and harps danced in the air; and there he was.

I remembered straight away, because I had that feeling of excitement that you only get when something is about to change your life.

Without breaking eye contact, he came over.
"This might sound crazy but I saw you a few months ago in Soho. You walked by in this black and white dress and I remember thinking you were the most beautiful girl I'd ever seen."

Oh babe...I remember.

He didn't need to know the amount of hours I'd spent searching for the beautiful brunette boy in Soho. Honestly, Google should pay me at this point.

"Oh yeah!" I said batting my long lashes. "I remember that dress."

We exchanged numbers and agreed to meet up after the movie. There was a pub around the corner that looked big enough for a party of ten to congregate.

I don't remember the movie but I remember the beers, the laughs, and the first kiss at the end of the night.

From that night, Rex and I were inseparable.

He lived in Notting Hill about thirty minutes away from me. We spent almost every night together, and the nights we didn't, we texted until we fell asleep.

One night, six months in, I had taken a break from a project to spend some time with Rex. Knowing how stressed I was, he'd cooked dinner and cleaned up afterwards while I relaxed with wine on the couch. Around eight thirty I said that I needed to go home as my presentation for work was weighing on my mind.

He came up behind me, gave me a kiss on the cheek and said, "Why don't you just move in?"

Everything stopped for a second.

I laughed, brushing the idea and my hair aside. Google always said that people who moved in before the one-year mark never made it.

"No. I want this to last," I said kissing him, "I'm here for the long run."

I moved in a week later.

The first few months were perfect. I would come home from work every night to a glass of wine and dinner on the stove. Not that Rex didn't have a job. He was an architect. But his family owned the company so he could come and go as he pleased. My PR job at a hotel wasn't as flexible but I loved it regardless.

Between coming with me to doctor's appointments, letting me have my Wednesday evenings with the girls, and starring on our man panel, it was becoming more clear Rex was perfect. We were going to be together forever. We did it all, the two of us. We shopped together, ate together, travelled together, slept together. Everything.

Another six months flew by. For our one-year anniversary, he took me to Nobu. There, his gift to me was a two week stay in Capri. Mine was an alpaca experience somewhere in the English countryside. It was cute, but I thought I enjoyed it more than he did. Soon after that, I started pinning wedding ideas. He loved the water, so I'd pin beach venues. He loved red wine, so I tasted every red wine known to man. He loved the colour blue, so my nails were always picture perfect in some shade of blue.

It wasn't that I was waiting, but I was going to be ready for the moment he asked.

It was smooth sailing until the storm came in the form of a late night phone call.

> "Mum?"
> "Em, Maddie's been in a serious car accident. They aren't sure if she's going to make it."

I booked a flight home that night.

As soon as I landed, I hopped in a taxi to town. The panic that arose in my chest was unbearable. I couldn't breathe. I couldn't think. All I could do was stare out the window. After an eternity, I arrived at Maddie's parents' house. There, I found out from Sandra and Mike that a car had hit Maddie when she was driving home from work late at night. She was barely alive when the ambulance had gotten to her.

For the next few weeks, I went between the hospital and my parent's house. I watched the days turn to nights in the hospital room by Maddie's side, telling her stories of our shared memories from the past 20 odd years together. Maddie was always there. No matter how much time or distance was between us, we always picked it up right where we left off. I couldn't imagine life without her, so I tried to take as much time as the universe would allow.

Rex made sure I was alright. He texted on WhatsApp every other day because he knew that I couldn't answer the phone in the hospital. He didn't ask me for rent. He didn't ask me for the bills. He just called to make sure I was okay.

Towards the end of the fourth week, she opened her eyes. At the end of the fifth week, she could sit up. The morning she sat up, when I opened the door, a small but present voice said, "Em what the hell are you doing here?" Maddie was smiling, sitting up in bed, surrounded by pillows.

I walked up to her and said seriously, "Remember when we made the pact in primary school that we would walk five hundred miles if we needed each other?" I gently held her hand, "Well I broke that promise. I didn't walk, I flew."

In the sixth week, she could sit up without support. In the seventh week, my job was starting to call asking when I would come back to London. In the eighth week after her accident, I left a voicemail for Rex.

"Hey, I'm coming home."
A few hours later he texted back, "Okay."
All I wanted was his familiar hug.

I finally flew back to London after two months in a hospital room. After the baggage claim, I waited at the terminal for an hour. I tried to call him, but it didn't go through. I figured there must be something wrong with my phone after switching SIM cards. I ended up getting myself an Express Train ticket and made my way back home.

When I opened the door, I was greeted with the smell of dust and stale air. Which was weird, because the place looked tidy as if he'd made an effort to impress me. But then, when I looked at things closer, there was a visible layer of dust over the kitchen table. Half of our things were missing. Our room was stripped of everything that had been his. There were no pictures. There was no TV. All of his clothes were gone.

I tried to make as many excuses for him as possible. The most logical being that there was a gas leak. The most extreme being that we had been robbed...but only his stuff had been taken. It made sense if you didn't think about it that hard.

I searched the house for an answer but there was nothing. I looked for anything: a letter, a note. Anything. Anything to know he was okay; that we were okay.

But there was nothing.

The only thing that was left was a can of tuna in the fridge. *How kind. Food, but no explanation.*

I called him once. No answer. I called him again. Still no answer. I must have called about 15 times. (Okay...it was 63, but who's counting?)

There was only one thing to do. Go buy two bottles of wine, sit in our empty home and eat that bloody can of tuna.

Two days went by in a blur I still don't fully remember. I couldn't sleep. I couldn't eat. The only response I got from anyone was that they 'didn't want to get involved' and how I should 'speak to him.' Well, I was trying, but his phone had been disconnected and he had blocked me on all social media.

On the third night, I got a call from a +246 number. Usually, I don't answer area codes I don't recognise because, as far as I know, I don't have any rich relatives who live in Barbados. This time, I said a quick Hail Mary and answered the phone.

"Rex?" I prayed into the phone.

"Hey Em."

My heart stopped.

"I'm so sorry. It has nothing to do with you," he tried to explain. "I'm in Barbados. They offered me a contract for building a new resort here. I couldn't refuse. I knew you were having a hard time and I didn't want to stress you out."

Yeah, because coming home to an empty home wasn't stressful.

"It's okay. I'm just glad you finally called and we can figure it out. I've never been to Barbados, I'm sure I would love it," I babbled, not feeling the burn on my wrist from twisting my bracelets too tightly.

"Em," he said softly.

"No, it'll be easy. I can work remotely. The hotel will understand. I can work part time here and part time at a hotel there. I can quit. I can just move there. There have to be hotels there who would value a London experience. Look, just let me look it up right now. I'm sure. Maybe even when your hotel is done. If we love it there, they can hire me. We can make this work."

"Em…"

"Please, please don't do this."

"…It's over."

Click

Well…that sucked...a lot.

But the worst part was that I had to move out of that beautiful Notting Hill detached house and into Riley's single room. Yes, I agree, it was too small for the two of us.

++

Three months later, on a Tuesday night, we were doing what every responsible adult does; stalk our exes, drink wine and eat a block of cheese...each.

It must have been predicted in the stars that something would have happened that night as we still had two bottles of wine left over when we were done.

The next morning, Riley woke me up with a leftover bottle and a curly straw.

"Babe," she said, "I'm gonna need you to drink most of this. I have something to tell you."

I took a big sip.

"Rex is engaged."

"What?"

"Yeah, it looks like they've known each other for a while. She's local in Barbados but she was in London for a holiday six months before he left."

I then proceeded to earn the world record for chugging a bottle of red wine at eight in the morning.

***

***

After the breakup with Rex, it took me some time to get back on my feet, find a new place to live, and feel a sense of purpose again. I didn't date for a while. Everything felt too raw- too soon.

It's been years now since Rex and I broke up. It took me a while to get over our story but I did with time. Within a year of his grand exit I had begun to form a new relationship with myself. After all, you are the one you end up with.

Besides, I had never just dated before. This was my chance.

At the end of the day, you have to decide to move on and give space for new stories because you never know who you are going to meet.

***

III
Old Photos

Wine Pairing: the accidental bottle of nonalcoholic wine your mom got you

***

I had been in this new flat ever since I had moved out of Riley's single bedroom after my breakup. I liked it, but there were a few issues. The heating never worked and sometimes the lights just went out.

Such was the case one day in June that I was, yet again, stuck in a dark flat. The only bright thing about the situation was my phone screen as I downloaded Tinder. Maybe the sparks from those virtual matches would bring some light into my dark shoebox.

In the dark with my phone at 13%, I agonised over every photo choice as my phone dwindled down to 5%.
Oh this one brings out the blue of my eyes! Adding...This photo with the next door neighbour's cat? Perfect. *What about this photo with the dog AND kitten from last Christmas? Even better.* (4%) *How about this one with when the girls and I went out for drinks that one night in February? No, the quality isn't as nice as the one from when we went to* (3%) *Paris for a weekend. That one! Friends and travel?* (2%) *Double yes. Alright...bio...hmmm it needs to show my wit.* (1%) *How hard can it be? I'm funny.... I just need to show them my unique personality...*

*Little spinning circle of death.

Okay, I'll just come back to the bio later. What do they say? A picture is worth a thousand words? Then, I have at least nine thousand words already.

The next morning, as the electricity was still not on, I went to my local cafe to charge my phone and get my morning coffee… okay really just to check Tinder. I had spent far too much time the night before wondering and dreaming about the hundreds of profiles I was going to get matched with: tall, dark and handsome strangers, all queuing up in this virtual world to meet me.

The phone turned on.

I manically put in my passcode and opened up Tinder. I was shocked there were zero matches before I remembered that I actually had to swipe right to get a match.

So I sipped my coffee and started swiping.

The first three were total duds. I was sure they were attractive to someone but that someone was not me. Then on the fourth guy we hit the jackpot. Tall - like, even I could wear heels next to him tall. Tattooed - I'm talking colourful double sleeves on well-formed arms. Dark features and a jawline designed to cut things. *Alright Jamie. It's your lucky day. I can't wait for this date.* *swipe right… *Huh? I guess it isn't instantaneous like I thought. I wonder how long I have to wait for there to be a match?*

Ten more swipe rights and no matches later, I started to worry that my profile hadn't been uploaded properly. The Tinder App Support number wasn't working so I thought I would test my theory out and swipe right on a left. I instantly matched with him.

Well, there was my lesson in humility for the day.

Three days and a few dozen matches later I felt like I finally had the hang of the whole Tinder thing. While I was still waiting for Jamie's match to come through (he clearly didn't use Tinder that often) I was matching with some interesting people.

Some of the profiles were intriguing; others were just different. This one had photos of him in Antarctica. This other one specified how much he liked coriander, not that there is a problem with liking coriander, but it seemed an odd fact to put on a dating profile. This one said he collected empty cans of beans from the 20th century: his top photo being his most valuable can from 1923.

From my four active conversations, my favourite was Jonathon. He was a 28-year-old banker from Australia who looked like a surfer god. Long sandy hair with sparkling ocean blue eyes that felt like I had to swim in them to get to the distant shores of his...beard. I had been to Australia once before for a month but wouldn't mind going back with a hot tour guide.

We exchanged messages at least once an hour. He was curious about me and asked me a lot of questions that ranged from the normal, ("*Where are you from?*") to the more personal, ("*How did your parents meet?*") to the flat out intense ("*What are your thoughts on collars*?"). I had never had someone that focused on me. It felt nice. But, about a month and a half into us talking, I realised I didn't know that much about him. However, he had somehow become one of my top three most frequently-messaged people on WhatsApp.

In the beginning of August, Jonathon went away to Dubai for business. I started to wonder if we were ever going to meet up. I had already been on a couple of failed Tinder dates with people who didn't excite me while I waited for him to come back. We still talked every day. I wasn't in love, but I did want to meet him.

He messaged me randomly one Friday afternoon to say he'd returned and wanted to take me out for dinner that night. It was sweet how he wanted to see me so soon after getting back but I had already made dinner plans with another striking gentleman from Tinder. However, we made plans to meet up late Saturday afternoon for dinner.

Unfortunately, I had to rearrange to the following weekend due to "food poisoning". Ladies, no matter how much the guy talks about his fantastic shots per game ratio, don't drink a bottle and a half of wine to yourself. And if you do, make sure you eat something before going to bed.

Throughout the week we continued to talk. He would tell me a little about his trip to Dubai if I asked, but mostly he was checking in to see how I was feeling. He was just thoughtful like that.

Finally, it was time for my date with the sexy surfer. After Facetime with Riley, Chanel, and Jess – to make sure my outfit was flawless – I left the house in a cute light summer dress and gold open-toed heels. Nothing beats a red dress on a first date.

I got to Hyde Park Corner five minutes early. I was starving. I hadn't eaten since lunch as we were going to a buffet. I messaged him to say that I was there and went to sit on a bench and people-watch in the sun while I waited. A couple seconds later he responded, "me too!" I looked around. There was no tall, blonde surfer god anywhere in sight. Trust me, I would have noticed him. The only people I could see were a young family admiring the rose garden, an older South Asian man sitting on the bench opposite me, a couple walking by (clearly on their fifth date), and a young woman running to catch the bus. The older South Asian man waved at me. I waved politely back while I looked at Google Maps to see if there was another station called Hyde Park Corner.

"Hi Em."

I looked up.

The older South Asian man was right in front of me.

"Jo...Jo...Jonathon?"

It took me a second to process what was going on.
Either he had lied – my memory was terrible – or I was in some
crazy dream. It wasn't like there were signs. I mean, I found it
weird how he never wanted to Facetime because of his "broken
camera" but, then again, some people are just camera shy.

My brain went into overdrive while he tried to explain
himself. He was the exact opposite of what he had put in his
profile. At least he had hair. It was longer than mine; a weird
choice to leave it down as it was so hot but...at least he had
hair.

"What happened?" I interrupted in a pure shock.
"Oh… those photos are really old," was his simple
explanation, said with so much confidence that I almost
questioned if I had in fact mistaken his photos.
*So, in five months you've changed from a tall, blond
Australian surfer to…* I thought to myself, but smiled at him in
confusion.
"But wha…." I started to say.
"So, shall we go?" he cut me off. "The buffet is right
around the corner…"

I stared at him.
*Is this guy out of his mind? Does he really think I'm
going to go with him after he so blatantly lied to me? Does he
think I'm blind? How stupid does he think I am?* I stood to
leave but as I felt faint from hunger, my starving stomach was
beating out my logical brain.

"Alright," I gave in as he led me to the buffet.

We got inside while I was still trying to figure out what
was happening. Before he would never talk about himself, but

now he wouldn't stop talking. To be honest, I had no idea what he was talking about. He mentioned something about a poison they'd found in some rocks in Russia. *Great. Now I can't even order a drink on this date.*

I opened up my phone to mine and the girls group chat.

Get the Wine

19:05 Em: I'm okay for right now, but man is this weird.
19:05 Jess: God okay, be careful.
19:06 Chanel: I hope you're eating all of the food
19:06 Riley: Hahaha but seriously, want me to send the cops to you?
19:06 Chanel: But actually
19:07 Jess: Message if you need us to come get you.

I was on the second plate when he said he had to go to the toilet. He came back when I was on my third. *What? If I couldn't drink for fear of being poisoned then I might as well eat all of the food.* He sat down grinning at me. I smiled back warily.

He leaned toward me and whispered, "Psst. Look what I grabbed." He opened his jacket to reveal three toilet rolls.

"Great. Now you don't need to stop at the shops later," I responded sarcastically, while thanking the universe it hadn't been some kind of flasher moment.

He laughed and closed his jacket, and noticed my nearly empty plate. "Good," he ejaculated, "you're eating a lot." He looked down at his own plate. "I like my women a bit bigger."

fork down *Oh hell no.*

I smiled as I pulled my phone out under the table and texted Jess.

19:37 Em: Call me. Get me the hell out of here.
19:37 *incoming call from Jess*

***

***

Obviously I deleted Tinder after that…

....and yes, I downloaded it again later.

***

IV

The Lock

Wine pairing: A bottle of the Riesling that I'm allergic to

***

Well...this is awkward.

I was on the toilet with my jumpsuit down to my ankles and three thoughts going through my mind:

1) How the hell do I get out of this situation?

2) How the hell did I get in this situation?

3)...

++

It all started when John texted me while I was getting ready for this particular Monday.

09:23 Unsaved number: "Hey, I know this is spontaneous but do you want to get dinner later today?"

"Riley," I called out. Riley had spent the night and was currently straightening her long hair in the washroom. "What was the name of the guy I gave my number to at the pub on Saturday?"

"Ummm," came Riley's response, "I think David or Conor or John or something like that…"

"OHHHH YEAH JOHN!"

I saved the number as John T to distinguish him from John M who was a guy from high school who occasionally visited London. The girls and I liked to joke that at the end of the world there would only be cockroaches and John M left, because the boy did not know when to give up. John T, on the other hand, I was glad to hear from.

John. John T. T for tall and handsome with curly dark hair and a five o'clock shadow that added a bit of roughness to his overall smooth appearance. He was, in other words, someone who I would gladly help repopulate the world with.

09:37 Em: Hey! My schedule today is a bit strange today. Can I let you know later?

The boss had told me to take a half day at the hotel because I had worked on the weekend which had left me drained. I wasn't exactly sure if I wanted to spend my energy on a date rather than at home where I could give myself a mini spa treatment and free home cooked meal.

After work I intended to come home to a nice hot bath and a glass of cold rosé. But when I had on my first face mask and looked in the fridge, I decided that a date was a good option as the only thing free in my fridge was space.

At 17:30 I rocked up to the place thinking about what I was going to order for dinner. Even in late-March, the weather was growing more cheerful with the sun smiling down on us cold and wet Londoners for the first time in months. Though possibly a premature celebration for the turn of the season, I decided to wear an open-backed yellow halter jumpsuit that mirrored the sun and was belted at the waist. To make it more casual and warm, I'd covered it with a jean jacket and cute boots.

I walked into the pub. It was a traditional English pub in Paddington with an open floor plan, tables along the edges and the bar in the middle of the room. Towards the back was the door to the garden and the stairs towards the toilets. Not seeing anyone I recognised, and with the pub looking rather full, I claimed the corner seats between the stairs and garden entrance. I put down my jacket on the seat and went to the bar.

"Hi," I said casually. "I was wondering if I could get a glass of Chardonnay and a menu please?"
"Chardonnay coming up," the barman said, getting out a glass. "But our kitchen is closed for the day. Sorry. We have pretzels."
"Oh, that's fine," I responded while my stomach grumbled. It appeared as though I was having a liquid dinner.

I took my glass and the pretzels back to my seat. As I was sitting down, I saw John walk in. He was even more handsome than I remembered. His light blue shirt accented his dark features in a way that made him look like a painting. That, combined with his beige trousers and brown shoes, showed that he took himself seriously and was not someone who would leave the toilet seat up in the house. *self high five.

"John! Over here!" I called out a little too excitedly. My heart skipped a beat as he confidently strolled over.
"Hi, Em," he greeted me. "I'm so glad you were free tonight. Whoa, love the jumpsuit. It's such a bold colour!
"Well, I didn't want you to miss me, so I thought I'd wear something eye catching."
"It worked!" he laughed, sat down and looked at my glass. "So, what are you drinking?"

The next two hours flew by. We talked about his interests in all things art, his favourite being artsy movies that showcase good design and storytelling- Hotel Budapest, in his opinion, being the best. He worked as an assistant director in an art museum in east London. After asking about my life growing up in Northern Europe, he told me how he had grown up in the north somewhere (I still wasn't well acquainted with England's geography and to be honest, I was distracted when he said exactly where because he had the audacity to ruffle his hair at that point). He had only moved to central London sometime a few years ago *What he was stretching*! but his abs...olutely loved it here.

We got along well. Several times over the date I thought about how happy I was I had decided to come out. I would still have to go to the shops afterwards, but it was so nice to talk to someone as interesting as him; it was even nicer to look at him.

"Haha cool. So, where did you grow up?"
|He looked at me with an eyebrow raised. "Still in Leeds…" he said jokingly.
"Haha oh yeah. No. Hah, I meant ummm. Where did you go to school?"
"Oh. Still Leeds." He laughed and leaned on the table. *Phew, saved it.*

I laughed as well in what I hoped was a flirtatious and cute giggle and playfully slapped his muscular forearm.
At this point, I was pretty hungry and had drunk two glasses of wine. While I was nowhere near tipsy, I did have to pee.

"Well," I said to him. "It's getting pretty late and I still haven't had dinner yet. I have no food at home, but was planning on stopping at the shops after this." I bat my eyelashes. "Do you have any interest in coming back to mine for some dinner?" I asked him confidently.

"Yeah. Sure. I'm pretty hungry. What do you have in mind?" he responded happily.

Thank God I hadn't eaten yet, I thought to myself as we discussed dinner ideas.

"So pizza. Awesome. I'm just going to use the ladies quickly and then we can go," I said, standing up.
"Great," he replied. "I'll be right here."

I made my way towards the toilets behind the bar but as I was about to reach the toilet door the barman stopped me, "Sorry miss, the female toilets are out of order. Just use the disabled toilet right by the garden door."

"I'm sorry, where is it?" I asked confusedly. He pointed back towards the direction of my table and said, "It's just by that table across from where you guys were sitting."

Great.

I made my way back to our table. John looked up at me, I shrugged and pointed towards the bathroom. "It was right here the whole time," I laughed awkwardly and quickly shut the door behind me.

I took the five steps to the toilet and hurriedly undid my jumpsuit. While I was sat on the toilet I pulled out my phone to look for the closest food shop.

Suddenly the door swung open.
"...in there…"
I looked up.

In front of me, a startled girl stood frozen with the door wide open. I locked eyes with John who, from his seat at the table directly behind her, could see me clearly. It was evident that he'd just tried to tell the poor girl I was in there but had been a bit too late. Unfortunately, the door was too far to close and the girl was too shocked to do anything.

1) How the hell do I get out of this situation?

2) How the hell did I get in this situation?

3) How do I look?

I awkwardly waved at him and looked back to the stammering girl.

"Ahh! Oh My God. I'm so so so sorry!" She said as she tried to close the door on my naked self.

"It's fine," I whimpered as I kept waving awkwardly at the two of them.

++

Needless to say, he did not come back to mine that evening. He got an emergency call from his brother who was 'locked out of his flat.'

"But I'll message you," he said.

I never heard from him again.

***

***

You learn from every experience. Safe to say that certainly was true for this situation. Even now I still double check that the door is locked.

***

V
Seabass

Wine Pairing: Chateau Margaux Grand Vin Margaux 90

***

It was one of those long weeks where everything was going wrong. At work, Amanda, one of my teenage interns, had taken Monday off due to 'stomach issues.' The heating had stopped working at home and I couldn't get the repair man in until next Tuesday. Plus, there was no proper food in the fridge because I was too exhausted after work to pick something up. On top of that, payday wasn't until the end of the month, so I had decided against takeout.

The only solution to the end of this horrible Wednesday was the cheapest bottle of wine, the not-so-cheap block of cheese, and to go to Jess's because her heating was working.

Get the Wine

14:03 Em: Jess, is your heating working?
14:06 Jess: Yeah. Yours still out?
14:10 Em: Yeah :(
14:16 Jess: :(Do you guys want to come over for a movie night?
14:22 Chanel: Yes please, today has been horrible
14:23 Em: :) YES
14:43 Riley: I can't. I have a date tonight with the army guy

---

Chanel and I arrived at the same time to Jess's house shivering and grumbling about our horrible days.

"My boss won't stop yelling at me about petty things. The Instagram post was one minute late. It was either going to be late or have a bunch of spelling mistakes because Amanda was hungover again and was hauled up in the bathroom for most of the day," I complained, as Jess opened the door in her workout leggings, her dark hair still up and sweaty from boxing class.

"Again? The girl needs to eat some toast before going to bed. That's the only way to not get a hangover."

"I know. I've told her, but she's nineteen and won't listen to anyone," I grumbled, momentarily forgetting my own self at nineteen. "It's just getting ridiculous at this point. She is so unprofessional and it's looking bad on me. But as the hotel owner's niece, she thinks she can do anything."

"That sucks," Chanel empathised with me while Jess handed us each a glass of wine as we made our way into the living room.

"I know. But at least she didn't puke all over the bathroom floor," I said, changing the conversation.

"OH GOD. Why did you have to remind me?" Chanel whined.

"What?" Jess gasped.

"Someone puked all over the bathroom today and since I'm the owner and the only other barista on duty was a sixteen-year-old trainee, I felt like I couldn't ask him to do it. So, I did. It was nasty."

"Nasty," I repeated as Jess lit some candles and selected *Bridget Jones' Diary.*

"Yeah, oh well. At least we have Bridget to commiserate with." Jess said pressing play.

We begin the movie.

"I wonder how Bridget's story might have changed if she had Tinder or Bumble?" Jess pondered as Bridget's mother fawned over Darcy on the screen while taking a bit of bread and dunked it in the fondue.

"Do you think she would have matched with Darcy instead of meeting him at the Christmas party?"

"Maybe," I respond, "depends on his photo selection and bio. She might have given him a chance."

We spent a few minutes imagining Darcy's prim-yet-boring profile.

"Or, or-" interjected Chanel, "or there would have been an interesting third guy for her to try and meet to get over Daniel."

"Yeah, but I doubt she would have found anyone good," I said nibbling on my bread. "None of these Tinder guys are worth it! They're all either asking for nudes in the first interaction or they're posing with a tiger. Like, why always a tiger picture from Thailand? If you really want to show me you're well-travelled, just give me your book selection," I muttered under my breath as I poured myself a second glass of wine.

"Em, you're too picky with your matches," Jess responded. "Before I met Will I used them and I definitely met some interesting people."

"Same. I've dated several nice guys from Bumble," Chanel added, adjusting her bluelight glasses while still watching the TV. "I mean, yeah, there are a few horrible guys, but you just learn to ignore and block them and remind yourself you don't owe them anything. You just got really unlucky with Catfish Guy." Chanel sipped her wine. "Instead of using your fake account to stalk Rex and his wife, you need to be spending that energy on meeting new people." We slipped back into silence as Bridget charted her cigarette intake.

"I just want to date right now," I voiced as Bridget finished her tub of ice cream.

"Give me your phone," Jess demanded.

"What?" I asked.

"Yeah. Let us use your Tinder and pick someone for you."

"YESS!" Chanel yelled excitedly, almost choking on her bread.

I looked at their pleading and excited faces.

"Sure." I unlocked my phone and handed it over to them.

While Bridget and Darcy made their blue soup, Jess and Chanel drooled over the guys on my Tinder. I made my way through my third glass of wine and helped myself to quite a lot of the bread and fondue, while occasionally glancing over to see who they were scouting out.

"Ooo, what about him? He went to Asia recently. He's well travelled," Jess and Chanel discussed as they analysed each profile together.

"No tigers!" I emphasised.

"There are no tiger photos," Jess promised as she kept scrolling through the profiles.

"That doesn't mean he doesn't have them." I protested.

"Em," Chanel warned as she pulled the phone away.

"Fine! But watch, he'll have a tiger photo that he shows me later. They always do. You can't go to a place that supports such animal cruelty just to get a good photo. You can't do that and still be a decent person. There is no in-between."

They kept swiping.

"Oh, this one has a lot of photos in New York. But he's only here for a little while."

"What about this one...why is there a girl? Oh, *oh*, okay. Um, this one is a couple looking for a third…"

Both of them looked up at me questioningly.

"Hmm, probably not for me," I said, casually drinking my wine.

"Oh. My. God," Chanel suddenly exclaimed. "This guy has a yacht!"

About ten minutes later, I took my phone back from my wing-women to inspect Yacht Guy. Based on his photos, he seemed to be about my height or a bit taller, medium build and blonde. His name was Edward. In his profile, he didn't have any social media accounts linked for "privacy" reasons. He listed his job as self-employed and an 'investor in solar energy.'

I swiped to the messages. Jess and Chanel had opened the conversation with him.

Tinder messages with EDWARD

Wednesday - 21:07

Em: Hey
Edward: Good evening! How are you doing?
Em: I'm fine. Just watching Bridget Jones' Diary with the girls. How about you?
Edward: What a classic. That sounds fun. Just having a quiet night at home.
Edward: I will let you enjoy your night with your friends and I will talk to you tomorrow.
Em: What a gentleman. Thank you. Have a nice night!

Over the course of the next two weeks, we talked fairly often. However, there were things about him that didn't make sense. He went on holiday a lot. He claimed to live in a castle in Kent which was rented out as a Bed and Breakfast. Finally, he kept talking about his estate. After analysing the situation with the girls, I realised it was too good to be true and there was no way I was going to get catfished again. So I decided to be mature about it and end things before they even started.

Wednesday - 13:06
Em: Meow
Edward: Excuse me?
Em: (fish emoji)
Edward: What?
Em: Meow?
Edward: I'm confused

Em: meow (fish emoji)
Edward: Wait hang on.
Edward: Are you calling me a catfish?
Edward: Do you really think I'm not who I say I am?
Em: There is only one catfish in this chat and it isn't me!
Edward: Do you think that I'm a catfish?
Em: Oh no! Of course not! If you don't hear from me for a while it's because I've gone to space to go get some rocks from Mars. It was nice to meet you "Edward"

Twenty minutes later accounts, linked to Edward R. S. followed me on all of my social media accounts. A few minutes after that, a castle's social media claiming to be the 'Finest and Oldest Bed and Breakfast in Kent' invited me to "like" them. A little while after that I got a notification saying that his solar energy company had sent me a personalised email. To cherry on top was his travel and food Instagram accounts requesting to follow me.

Damn it.

That evening, we met at Chanel's cafe before going to the Cinema.

"I might have jumped to that conclusion too quickly," I said to Riley while we were waiting for Chanel to close up the cafe.

"This is really bad."

"I know. I feel so horrible," I responded, putting my head in my hands. "But you know why I thought he was a catfish."

"I know, Em, but how often does the same person get catfished twice? I can understand why you felt like that, but you were brutal and really immature with this guy!" she responded, staring in shock at the phone. Then she stifled a laugh and said to me, "You have two options: ignore him forever, or call him and explain."

"I know, but I'm too ashamed now."

"Em…" she said as she blocked my phone from my view.

"Riley," I said hesitantly. "What…"

The phone started buzzing

"What did you do?"

"Nothing! He's calling you."

"WHAT?"

"Answer it!"

"Hello? Sorry Em, I missed your call. I thought I was never going to hear from you again," came a voice across the phone.

"Hi. Hold on one second."

I got up, giving Riley a glare as I walked out. Chanel's cafe along the South Bank was a chic and stylish little space right next to the river. It had been open for a year now and was starting to become a local favourite for the neighbourhood. Outside, I stood next to the river in the mid-March chill, trying to compose myself.

"Hey, I'm back. Sorry about that, I didn't really expect you to call back." I paused waiting for a response that never came. I took a deep breath and continued, "Umm, no, I actually wanted to apologise for how I spoke to you. I've a bad experience with a catfish so I'm extra cautious now."

"Cautious? Paranoid more like it," he laughed. "But on a serious note, I am sorry. I can see why you would think what I'm saying might not be true. How about we settle this debate once and for all on Friday. Text me your address and I'll take care of the rest. Just be ready by seven."

He abruptly hung up the phone.

Well, that was a dramatic ending.

That following week was a very productive week at work; I decided on five solid topics that anyone could easily talk about; I played out every possible scenario in my head; I primped and waxed everything that needed to be primped and waxed; I bought new lipstick; and I even chose my perfect outfit.

Turns out, I didn't need to worry about the outfit. On Wednesday, he posted me a dress. It was the blackest of blacks, long with a mini train and a deep v in the back. The beautiful bell sleeves made me feel like a movie star about to walk on a red carpet.

It was quite flattering that he thought I could fit into a size 6. *God bless you Spanx.*

Wednesday - 19:31

Em: Thank you for the dress. It's so beautiful!
Edward: Glad to hear. Does it fit alright?
Em: Perfectly!

With the help of the girls I was ready on time. In the end we went with a 1940s Hollywood glam makeup with bold red lips and dramatic eyes and gold bangles to set off the black.

Besides a fishing trip, I was ready for anything.

It was 18:45 on Friday evening and it was getting harder and harder to breathe...not just because the spandex was cutting into my diaphragm but also because my nerves were through the roof.
To calm myself, I opened a bottle of sparkling wine. It didn't do much for my breathing as I just got more bloated but I did feel more relaxed...so it kind of did its job.

At exactly 19:00 on the dot, my doorbell rang. I grabbed my coat and opened the door.

A serious man in a suit was standing there.

Well, aren't you a pretty catfish, I thought to myself. "I knew it. Well done Edward. You got me," I said out loud.

"No, ma'am. I'm just the driver. Your car is waiting outside. Please follow me."

"Oh," I said as I peered around him to the Bentley he was pointing at.

He escorted me to the car, opened the door for me, and I got in.

Thirty minutes and two glasses of complimentary champagne later, we pulled up outside a members-only club in SOHO. A different man in a tux came out to open my door and help me out. I felt like I was a princess in a fairytale.

This night is going to be magical, I mused to myself as I stepped out of the car.

I walked up the stairs on the red velvet carpet that led through the impressive doors into a white marble atrium that had a grand staircase leading to the first floor. Surrounding the big pillars that supported the low ceiling were green plants to add some life to the room. The aroma of fresh flowers floated in the air from the white lilies by the door.

The kind girl manning the cloakroom took my trench coat with a smile. I walked up the stairs to meet a second man in a tux standing by a slightly less impressive set of doors, who then asked me who I was with.

"I'm waiting for someone named Edward," I responded while still taking in the glamour around me.

"Very well, his Lordship is just over behind the trees. I will take you to your private dining room."

"His what?!"

"His private dining room, ma'am. Please, follow me."

Okay, Tux Man, I joked with myself as a way to calm my nerves while he led me through the door.

Inside was darkly lit with low burning chandeliers that gave the illusion of being inside the flame of a candle. The gentle light gleamed off mahogany panelling and glinted off the golden details of the maroon wallpaper that spun and circled their way up to the high, overarching ceilings. The room was full of people sat at tables, laughing politely at jokes that weren't that funny, smiling over the romantic courses, and looking like they had just come out of a museum painting.

The only place I felt I truly belonged was amongst the velvet chairs. It was almost uncanny how my dress matched them so perfectly. Tux Man led me down the crimson path towards the back of the restaurant, past a line of trees that looked and smelled as if they had been transplanted from the south of Spain, to a big black door with gold door handles.

"His Lordship is just through here, ma'am," Tux Man announced. "Is there anything I can bring you?"

"Um. Water would be great. Thank you," I stammered as I stared around me. I reached for the door to go in.

"Still or sparkling, ma'am?" Tux Man inquired.

I froze.

"Still, thank you."

"We have several options, anything specific?"

"No. Um, any water is good," I responded nervously, not sure how there could be multiple options for water.

"Very well ma'am. Would you like a tall or short glass? Garnish?"

MY. GOD.

"A tall glass would be great."

"Very well." He opened the door for me.

Dear Lord, this water had better taste freaking amazing.

I walked into a warm room lit by a blazing fire. It felt as if I had stepped back in time. The walls were covered in the same deep maroon wallpaper as outside but with black designs that accentuated the richness of the rouge. The crystal chandelier dangling from the ceiling was more for decoration than for light as the weak reflection of each tiny bulb danced about on the table in the middle of the room. At the back stood Edward, looking out of a window, in a black tux and black velvet shoes...*obviously*.

He turned around holding a whiskey on the rocks in a short glass.

"Hello, darling. You look ravishing. I'm so glad to see you on this fine evening," he said in a pleasant tenor voice as he came over, extended his hand, and kissed me on the cheek.

If drama could be shown as a picture in the dictionary...it would be this.

"Good evening," I said, overwhelmed by the whole scene. Accepting his hand, he led me to a low sofa in front of the fireplace.

"I hope it is okay, but I have selected the courses for tonight," he said as we sat down. "Please don't feel the need to eat anything you are not comfortable with as I rudely forgot to ask if you had any dietary restrictions."

"Don't worry. I eat everything. Just think of me as a food composter."

Edward laughed politely while giving me a curious glance. Tux Man reappeared and brought me my tall glass of still water without garnish.

"Here you are, ma'am. Is there anything else I can get for you? Or," he asked, turning to Edward, "would you like a bottle of your favourite?"

"Yes. We will have the Chateau Margaux Grand Vin Margaux, Gregory. Also, another whisky on the rocks. Short glass. No garnish."

"Yes, sir." Gregory gave a small bow and walked out.

"So what do you think of the place?" he asked me as he scooched closer. I was looking out into the dark night on what I could only assume was the back of a private garden. The lights outside were shining through the London fog and made the whole atmosphere feel like I'd stepped into 1875. It felt luxurious and romantic...or weird. I hadn't quite decided yet, but I definitely wasn't feeling comfortable.

"It reminds me of something out of a book," I responded while I played with my gold bracelet and looked back at him.

"Excellent. My family have been members of the club for generations. They have a lovely spa downstairs that my mother would go to while my father and I would come here in the summer for a drink. There is a billiards room on the second floor which is where he taught me everything I know. I will show you around sometime, but probably not tonight," he said.

"I would love that," I replied, leaning in a bit closer. He had marvellous, dark green eyes. "Do you see your family often?"

"No. They spend a great deal of time at the manor house in Nice. My sister and her family spend most of their free time at the family house in Tuscany because it has a beautiful pool that the kids can enjoy. So, I get to spend most of my free time at the family castle in Kent and stay at the townhouse in Mayfair when I have business in London."

"Oh," I said, trying to process this information. I took an indulgent sip of my still tasteless water. "I've never been to Italy, but I would love to go for the wineries."

He smiled politely as the door opened and Gregory brought us our wine.
"It is the 1989 bottle, sir. Would you like a taste?"
"Yes, we will both have a taste."
Gregory unscrewed the cork, placed it on a little side plate and handed it to Edward. I thought it was odd till he took a big sniff of the cork...that I just thought it was strange.

Meanwhile I had taken the glass that was offered to me and threw it back.

"Wow, that is so good!" I cried in ecstasy.

Gregory's face was aghast while Edward laughed.

"We are going to have fun tonight. You aren't like the other girls I bring here. Is she, Gregory?"

"No, sir," he replied. "She is not."

Feeling a blush creep up my cheeks from Gregory's harsh stare, I turned quietly back to the fire.

"The first course will be ready in a few minutes," said Gregory. "Would you like to be seated now?"

"Yes. Thank you, Gregory." He stood up from the sofa. "Come, Em, let's go to the table."

Watching Edward walk away, Gregory coldly asked, "Your drink, ma'am?"

"Oh yes. Of course," I said. He turned around and I went to follow him for my drink. After a few paces he turned around, startled. "No ma'am. I will bring you your drink."

"Oh." I quickly turned towards the table as Edward pulled the seat out for me.

"What did Gregory want?"

"Huh?" I asked trying to win a few seconds to come up with a reasonable and less embarrassing answer.

"Just now. Were you scared you weren't going to get your wine?" he smiled.

"No...I…"

"It's okay. I can understand. This is so different from anywhere else you have probably been to before. I can imagine how overwhelming it must be. But please don't go up to the kitchen to pick up the first course, I think Gregory would have a heart attack!"

I laughed and ignored the slight while swallowing my wine.

Honestly, never have I ever tasted wine that was as smooth or as rich.

I'm going to have to remember this bottle.

"So, where else have you not gone?" he asked presumptuously.

I looked at him in confusion. Not knowing how to answer it, "Well, I want to go to the Caribbean next summer with my friends. My friend Chanel's parents were one of the founders of Carnival here in Lon…."

"Oh, you will love the Caribbean. I can't believe you have never been. I go there twice a year at least! It is so nice to escape the London cold and be somewhere warm. I go to this resort in Jamaica that my father helped invest in in the 1970s. So we always have space in the Manor House Suite for whenever we want to go. One time I forgot to ring them up, you know, too many glasses of Dom on the jet, so my ex-girlfriend and I showed up and they had to kick out this family. It was the funniest thing. If you go there, make sure you use my name at reception...you're welcome in advance for the treatment you girls get."

I looked at him with what must have seemed like a look of admiration but was, in reality, a look of *what the hell is this shit?*

He went on to talk about his model ex-girlfriend, whose father had invented a particular screw that was only used in expensive cars and made out of a mixture of platinum and gold.

"Wow. That is one fancy screw," I joked as I drank more of the wine.

"Well, it's actually terrible for the environment," he responded, bypassing my eloquent and lady-like joke. "What he should have done is changed how he makes the screws so that they're…"

"Excuse me, sir, I'm sorry to interrupt but..."

"Yes, Gregory what do you want?" Edward rudely interjected, clearly angered at being interrupted, which seemed out of character as he didn't seem to mind interrupting me.

"Your first course will be here momentarily. However, we have run out of the seabass for your third course. I'm not sure where the mix-up was, but they seem to have given the last of it to the room next door," Gregory explained.

"Well, I'm sure you can arrange something, Gregory," Edward smiled expectantly. "As you know, my family has done so much for this establishment."

"Yes, sir, however it might take another hour before we can get any more seabass in. And then, we cannot guarantee that it will be to the same quality or standard we are accustomed to," Gregory responded.

"You will figure it out, I'm sure, Gregory," he replied with a reptilian smile. "We will be having the seabass."

"Thank you, sir."

"And while you are at it, please bring us another bottle of wine. As you can see, our glasses are rather empty," Edward demanded, tapping his glass with two fingers.

I looked at him rather surprised, as I'd only started my second glass. But he was right; the bottle was indeed almost done. How he'd had the time to drink more than I had while telling me all of those opulent stories was beyond me.

"Damn, I need to catch up," I said to him, pointing to my wine glass as Gregory left.

"Oh, don't worry. I can order us ten more bottles if you want. Enjoy your wine at your own pace," he said, waving my statement aside like it was an annoying fly. I was sure he was trying to sound kind, but it came out pugnacious.

The second course was accompanied by more bottles of wine. I wasn't sure where all the wine had gone but I was certain I had found my match...in wine drinking. I wasn't totally convinced that Edward was a nice person. His manner and behaviour were so rude and crass that it didn't matter if he was. From his ever-so-kind offer for me to stay at his Jamaican suite to the invitations for weekends away in their home in the alps for ski season (which rubbed me the wrong way, because, well...just because I was from Finland doesn't mean I love skiing), to his declaration that we were going to spend a week on his yacht in the Mediterranean in June, Edward just kept talking. I don't know how he managed to finish three bottles of wine by himself without my help. Even with taking a sip every time he mentioned the words 'estate,' 'solar,' 'manor', or 'unfair taxes' I only finished one and a half bottles myself.

While we were waiting for Gregory to come back from his fishing trip to the canal, I excused myself to go to the toilet. Like everything else in the club, the ladies' toilets were spectacular. The basins were made of gold with leaf faucets that didn't make sense but looked so beautiful. The walls were a black marble like the door at the front of the private club. There was a small cream couch at the end of the powder room (yes, there was a powder room) that must have been for fancy ladies in too-tight corsets or for women who were on dates as bad as mine – both about equally as painful.

Get the Wine

20:43 Em: I can't do this anymore! He is an arrogant son of a bitch. He won't stop talking about himself.
20:44 Chanel: Stay for the wine!
20:44 Riley: STAY FOR THE STORY!

As I made my way across the crimson carpet towards our private dining room, I could hear yelling. Suddenly, Edward threw open the door.

"Come, Em! We are leaving. We are NOT staying in this establishment," he turned, looking at a man I hadn't seen before who I assumed was the manager of the club. "You will be hearing from my father about this," he proclaimed threateningly.

"Sir, again, we are sorry that the celery was on your plate," he said, clearly exasperated by the situation. "It was an honest mistake. The chef is new. He doesn't know your preferences."

"Fine," Edward huffed as he composed himself. "But I will not be returning until he is gone." He turned to me. "Em, let's go."

He grabbed my hand and dragged me towards the cloakroom. I turned, baffled, towards the waiter and I mouthed, "I'm so sorry," and shrugged. The whole restaurant was looking at us from behind their menus. Once again, I noticed how I matched the interior, but this time it was from the burning on my cheeks, rather than the velvet of my dress.

Edward pulled me behind him as he speed-walked down the stairs.

"My coat!" he barked drunkenly at the poor girl behind the counter.

She looked at him in shock and confusion.

"I'm sorry, sir...What is…"

"NOT SIR. I AM A LORD AND YOU WILL CALL ME 'YOUR LORDSHIP'."

I looked at him in pure shock. Lord or not, I was not letting anyone talk to a woman like that. I pulled my hand out of his, looked her square in the face and said "I'm sorry for my date's rudeness. It's our first and only date."

**

"What do you mean it's our 'only date'?" he slurred to me, smelling like old whiskey and expensive cologne as he swayed to and fro on the pavement outside the club.

"Listen. We're so different. It's not going to happen," I explained, while looking for the Uber I had ordered inside.

"But I paid for dinner."

I ignored him.

"Fine, let's make tonight count then." He leaned in to kiss me but I ducked out of the way disgusted.

"First of all, you didn't pay. Second of all, even if you did. I still don't owe you anything."

The Uber pulled up; I opened my own door.
"Goodnight, *your lordship*," I said as we pulled away.

Get the Wine

21:22 Em: Girls, get the wine. Are you still at Riley's. I have so much to tell you...I'll be there in 30 minutes
21:25 Riley: WHAT HAPPENED??
21:27 Riley: RED OR WHITE?
21:27 Jess: Cheese? Do we need cheese?
21:33 Chanel: I'll slice the bread.
21:35 Jess: I'll get your PJs
21:39 Em: Thank the Lord it's Friday.

***

***

The dress is still hanging in my closet somewhere. You never know when you might need to be fancy. A duke might ask me to be his plus one at a wedding.

***

VI

They Ran out of Asparagus

Wine Pairing: A mini bottle of £2 white wine from the supermarket

***

In my opinion, Summers in London are unmatched. The cold that has impacted the rest of the year dispels briefly, allowing all of London's inhabitants to remove their cold exteriors and bask in the warmth of the sun. Biking past the different parks, you could find people with raised glasses to toast to the magnificent weather and the longer days. There was a general happiness the whole of London could suddenly feel. It was on one such Saturday afternoon that saw me waddle my way to meet the girls for a fancy dinner in Central London.

The restaurant was noisy as I struggled with the door. From down below, I could hear the sound of the band playing but I was too busy heaving four overflowing bags into the small waiting area. I tried to ignore the stares of the people drinking their wine on the patio as I looked around for the host like it was normal to stand over a mountain of frozen food and other groceries in the front of a fancy restaurant. The host came out with a benign smile on his face.

"Good evening," he said emotionlessly, "can I help you with…" he looked down and stopped talking, clearly unsure of what help he could offer.

"Actually, I'm meeting my friends here; I believe the booking is under Chanel. Obviously I have a bit of a baggage problem." I tried to sound confident while gesturing to the pile of falling over bags. The host looked at me with an eyebrow raised so I continued hurriedly, "It is a long story. Do you have a fridge where I can leave all this food?"

"I'm afraid not," was his blank response, "but we do have a cloakroom."

Five minutes later, I walked down the spiral stairs to the dining area where the others were sitting. Before I even saw them, I heard a roar of laughter. The girls were sitting on the far side of the room near the dance floor. As I approached them, Riley, in her white lace dress that complimented her tan and newly brown hair, was at the end of telling a story that seemed to have the other girls captivated.

"And then he had the audacity to say, 'females can't be lawyers.' Obviously I was out the door thirty seconds later."
"Good on you!"
"He didn't try to stop you and apologise?"
"Well, before he could try, I was already packing my things. Besides, I couldn't care less. I wasn't going to give him a second more of my time where he could insult me."

"Em!" Chanel said, catching sight of my sweaty face, "What happened to your date? You got here quickly." She flicked her braids behind her.
"Yeah. We weren't expecting you to get here till we got dessert," Jess noted looking down at her watch.
"Bad date?" Riley asked sympathetically while eating her chips. Without saying anything she passed her wine to me.

I gratefully took the glass, "You would not believe what just happened." I took a big sip and then launched into my story.

++

Earlier this week I got a very nice and polite DM on my Instagram. Usually I don't respond to them but the person seemed to be genuinely interested in my unique pictures and appreciated the funny captions. After doing a little bit of research on his profile, I found that he was single and pretty cute- so I decided to respond.

Instagram Direct Messages

Monday 07:11

Unforgettablesalad101: Hello beautiful, I know you probably get a lot of these. I am sorry for the random DM slide but your photos really caught my eye and your captions got my laugh. It is amazing how someone so lovely can also be so witty. I hope you have a nice day, gorgeous.
EmEmEm: Aw thank you! I love your food pictures. They make me drool!

Over the next few days we had a nice casual chat. He seemed a bit socially awkward at times but he was very polite. To be honest, when the conversation ever lacked, we talked about our favourite foods. You know, some people talked about the weather- we talked about food. So when he asked me about my favourite supermarket, I didn't think it was strange.

Instagram Direct Messages

Thursday 21:01

Unforgettablesalad101: What is your favourite supermarket?
EmEmEm: Oh, you know, Marks and Spencers or Waitrose when I'm feeling fancy. The big Tescos when it is past 23:00 but in general I go to the Sainsbury's by my house. They have an awesome cheese isle!
Unforgettablesalad101: Cool. What are your thoughts on Whole Foods?
EmEmEm: Ummmm that it's expensive? Haha

Unforgettablesalad101: Yeah. hahah What do you normally get in the shops?

What do I normally get at the shops? How do I answer that? That's a good, albeit random, question. Ummm haha OH YES! I'll send a screenshot of my shopping list. He'll find that hilarious. Upload...sending...SENT.

I laughed at my funny idea. However, he didn't reply till the next morning. But he did ask me to go on a date the following Saturday.

Get the Wine

13:34 Chanel: It looks like it will be nice out tomorrow! We have to do something.
13:55 Riley: Yes, but it's a bit too hot for a picnic. Let's go somewhere nice and then go out in the evening, I really wanna dance.
14:03 Jess: Yesss. I've got 2 more weeks of the school year and I can't be asked to cook for myself.
14:10 Chanel: Great. There is this restaurant near Piccadilly Square I've been wanting to try.
14:11 Jess: Oh! That place is so good. Will took me there. Let's do that.
14:15 Em: Perfect, that's where Supermarket Guy wants to meet. Unless things go REALLY well, I'll meet you there afterwards.

Since it was Saturday and I knew that I was meeting up with the girls after the date, I thought it would be a good opportunity for a 'me day.' and decided to go to the gym. After a rigorous 15-minute walk on the treadmill, I figured that was enough for me to reward myself with their sauna.

When I was done, I walked home to get ready for my evening. Outside it was beginning to cool off but the sun was still shining high in the sky around 16:00. With Coldplay blasting in my ears I took the long way home to enjoy my favourite season in London.

On the way, I stopped in a pharmacy to buy some face masks to enjoy as I picked out an outfit while continuing to listen to my summer playlist. I hadn't been on a proper date with a nice gentleman in a hot minute so I wanted to make an effort. As it was such a lovely day, I decided on a white silk skirt with a white lacy bodysuit underneath. For some drama, I added my signature gold jewelry and picked nude heels that tied up around my ankles.

I have a bit more time. Hmm might as well curl my hair.

Thirty minutes before we were set to meet, I hopped on the tube to get to Piccadilly Square. As I arrived a bit early, I sat next to the fountain and watched as the street performers danced to pop music in front of me.

*Ding

Instagram Direct Messages

Saturday 17:01

Unforgettablesalad101: Hey, I know we said to meet at the square, but could you actually come around the corner to meet me? *Send screenshot of map
EmEmEm: Sure.

I stood up, checked that my skirt was still clean, and then went to cross the street. All around me, London's signature black cabs drove by as big red busses stopped for yellow lights.

I ended up on a quiet side alley that, unless I had been using the map he sent me, I never would have found.

There was only one other person near me. At the end of the street, between two parked cars, I saw a man. I assumed it was my date as who else would be standing and waiting on this small street. I quickly took him in while walking towards him. He was tall- actually very tall- lanky, ashy hair, and wearing sunglasses. He seemed to be in his early 30s and clearly was coming from the supermarket as he was surrounded with large bags of groceries.

Thank God I put in some effort on my outfit. Look at that suit! But how is he wearing all black? It's so hot. Oh look at that waist coat and...is that a silk tie? Bit strange he brought his food shop on our date.

We locked eyes. He took off his sunglasses and put them in his pocket.

"Hi, it's nice to meet you," I said as I drew closer and leaned in for a hug.

That hug wasn't successful as he suddenly fell on his knees and sank into a low bow with his hands out in front of him. It was lucky we were on an abandoned ally or else people might have stopped to stare at me- wondering what kind of person I was to make someone bow at my feet.

"Your groceries," he said in a servant like manner, his face still on the ground.

"Excuse me?!" I exclaimed in pure shock. Was I more shocked by him being on the hot ground for this long or for the amount of food he was kneeling with? I don't think I'll ever know.

"I got everything on your list. Except for the asparagus. Sorry. They ran out of asparagus."

The girls laughed hysterically as my story drew to a close. Gasping, Jess looked at me in disbelief as she wiped her teary eyes. On either side of her, Chanel and Riley sat doubled over in their chairs clutching at their sides with laughter.

"Honestly, I thought our food and supermarket conversation were an original, but odd, ice breaker. Of course I sent the list as a joke- not an actual food order. Since he's commented on my sense of humour, I thought he would find it funny. Never in a thousand years did I think he would actually go and buy the whole list."

"So what about the rest of the date?" Chanel asked. The others tried to contain their laughter so they could listen to the rest of the story.

"There wasn't one. He just slowly got up off of the ground, didn't make eye contact, and almost ran away leaving me with the four bags of groceries in the middle of the alleyway. I mean, I think I stood there longer trying to figure out what to do next than I was on the actual date," I said in a tone that showed that I was still clearly confused about the whole situation.

"What did you do with all of it?"

"Oh. Um. I carried all the food here. It's in the cloakroom upstairs." I laughed as I realised the absurd reality of it all.

"You left them where?" Riley asked in disbelief as Jess and Chanel shook with renewed laughter.

"What? It's not like I could just bring them with me to the table," I protested. "And I wasn't about to make the trek to and from Chelsea to drop them home and get back here to meet you guys two minutes from where I had my ...delivery," I said as I crossed my arms.

"Oh my God." Riley said with a laugh.

We joked and ate our way through the rest of the night. The band was starting to play as couples made their way to the floor to dance to Big Band classics. When we had finished our meal we began planning on what to do next.

"So, should we stay for one more drink?" Riley posed to us after the waitress asked if we wanted anything else.

"Sure. Another one sounds good."

"Yeah, we could always go next door later. I love their vibe and I really want to dance tonight."

"I'm easy, doesn't matter to me."

"Girls," I cut in, "I still have all that food upstairs..."

***

***

The art of the DM Slide. Sometimes they can be entertaining. Sometimes they can be interesting. Sometimes they can completely backfire… Literally

***

VII

Spices and Bubbles

Wine Pairing: La Marca Prosecco

***

Do you ever have those mornings when you can hear the birds outside, the sun is shining through your blinds, the air is warm, promising a hot day, but you're too hungover to appreciate it?

That was us on this particular morning. It was one of the last few days of the summer holidays. To celebrate Jess's last few nights of freedom we had decided to make the most of it by having a proper night out, dancing the night away before she went back to work for the Autumn term.

I felt someone stir next to me. I rolled over and there was Jess, or what was left of her.

"Jess, do you want water?" I whispered, attempting to sit up.

Jess mumbled and rolled over. There was a soft fart noise from her side of the bed. "Sorry," she murmured. "That's what you get for making too much noise; now shush."

I would have laughed but my head was pounding.

Those three vodka tonics, two gin and sodas, and four glasses of wine with dinner, followed by one-too-many hours on a dance floor were starting to seem like a bad idea. We lay in bed for a few more hours, trying to put the pieces of our broken bodies back together, nurture our tired souls, and surprise our overworked livers with some water.

That article I read that said organic wine doesn't give you a hangover lied.

"Is it time to do the damage check?" Jess asked quietly.

I rolled over. "Alright," I sighed, preparing myself for the cringe. We simultaneously reached for our phones.

Aside from the normal Instagram and Snapchat stories of drunk girls screaming off pitch words of their 'favourite song ever', there wasn't too much damage; Jess had sent a few entertaining drunk texts to her boyfriend, and on my end, there were no messages sent to the FNC list and, most importantly, no messages in response to 'his lordship' (or as we liked to call him, the current king of the clowns).

We both heaved a sigh of relief and began to think about getting out of bed to slowly start the rehumanisation process.

By three o'clock, we had successfully moved our tired bodies onto my living room couch and ordered ourselves a McDonald's.

*ding

Instagram Direct Messages

15:11

URCarribeanAverageJoe: "Umm sorry...Do I know you?"

I looked at Jess with a puzzled expression. "Did I give someone my Instagram last night?"
Jess concentrated hard while thinking back to the blurriness of the night before. "Um, no, I don't think so. But I

did leave you unsupervised for a few minutes when I went to get us more drinks."

In absolute fear and dread, with a twist of curiosity, I opened the messages on Instagram.

We looked at each other in horror.

"YEEHAW Cowboy?!" I read aghast at my late-night messages. "What was I drinking last night?"

"My question is," Jess giggled, "why did you send 17 cowboy emojis? Like, why 17? Are they…they're ten minutes apart! How...?"

"I don't know, ask Drunk Em!" I said in a high pitched screech.

"Don't talk about alcohol right now," Jess moaned as she winced at my sudden outburst. "My stomach can't handle anything. Shoot. It says you've seen it. He's typing!"

"What's he saying?"

Instagram Direct Messages

15:33
URCarribeanAverageJoe: Hello? Cowgirl?
EmEmEm: Hi, yes. Have you seen my horse? I appear to have lost it and my whole team seems to be missing as well.
URCarribeanAverageJoe: Hahaha brilliant.
URCarribeanAverageJoe: No, I haven't seen it.
URCarribeanAverageJoe: But I'll keep my eye out for him.
EmEmEm: Thank you. We are all very worried.

I exited the messages.

"Thank God he can take a joke," I said to Jess, who was now lying next to me on the couch with a water bottle in one hand and her McDonald's in the other.

"Was he cute?" she asked back, staring at the ceiling.

"I'm not sure. Most of his pictures had a few people in it."

Putting down the water bottle, she put her hand out expectantly. I gave her my phone.

We sat in silence for a few minutes while Jess did her thing and I stared into the abyss, unable to move without wanting to vomit. I sipped my lemonade and debated if it was a good idea to get a second burger; my stomach was definitely still feeling the damage of the organic wine.

Jess gasped.

"What? Is he married?" I asked in a panic. "Is he under house arrest? Don't tell me: he's another lord!"
"This picture from his Aunt Carol's wedding from 2016. I want to get married here." she exclaimed, showing me a family photos of Joe's. I relaxed and ordered my second burger using Jess' phone.

15 minutes later, Jess looked up as I came back with my snack. She put the phone down, folded her hands, and began her briefing.

"His name is Joseph, after his Grandpa, but he goes by Joe. I think this was probably so that he didn't get confused when he was little. He went to a primary school called St. Gilbert's and then went on to an all-boys' school called St. Helena's (why an all-boys' school was named after a female patron saint, I don't know but that's a different conversation).

"He then left the Caribbean for university in the States when he was 18. He had two girlfriends at UPenn; Chakira and Mariana - both stunning. He seems to be about 6'2 as Mariana is wearing heels in three photos he's posted and he's still significantly taller. It looks like Chakira and Joe are on good terms as they still follow each other, but I don't know what happened with Mariana. His photos with her are still up but there are none tagged of him from her.

"He emigrated to the UK for grad school about 8 years ago and has been consulting for Bit Company Ltd since he graduated. Since being here, he seems to have had one serious girlfriend, Hanna. He was definitely reaching because she was GOR-GEOUS. He was tagged in her family's Christmas card three years ago and, let me say, her family cannot produce anything less than an eight.

"Joe and Hanna appear to have broken up about a year ago and he seems to have been enjoying the single life ever since, so you haven't done anything wrong." Jess picked up her bottle to take a drink. She continued, "His handle might be CaribbeanAverageJoe but he is definitely not average. Good job."

This, ladies and gentlemen, is probably the greatest benefit of having Jess as one of your best friends. Honestly, I still think she missed her true calling of being a private investigator.

I put my phone on charge, turned myself into a human tortilla under a blanket and took a bite of my burger.

Two days later, while I was at work, I received another message from Joe.

It was a horse emoji followed by, "Hi, is this your horse?"

I smiled into my phone and typed back.

My heart flipped. I typed back quickly.

The next three days we sent casual and flirty messages
to each other. He was smart, polite, and incredibly built, almost
like a statue. Since I knew the majority of what he had to tell
me, I tried to ask questions to things I didn't know the answers
to. We ended up talking about what we studied at Uni (science),
our favourite holidays (Summer Solstice, which isn't a holiday

but he argued was still the best day of the year), the names of our future pets (Catthew and Grey-ham) and our London bucket list (eating all the bagels in Brick Lane). It was safe to say, I was excited for this date.

I picked out my favourite outfit of the moment – a matching navy blue trouser and blazer set – and paired it with a white silky top and my bright red "get it girl!" heels. I felt powerful and sexy.

At 19:52, I arrived and was pleasantly surprised to find him already there waiting for me next to the restaurant door.

"I only got here a few minutes ago," he said as he gave me a kiss on the cheek. He smelled amazing. "They'll be ready for us in 10 minutes. You look beautiful."

I blushed and thanked him. He looked good. What is it about boys and their ability to only wear a simple shirt and dark jeans but somehow still look amazing? In this case, was it the fact you could see Joe's well-defined abs through his shirt? We'll never know but all I could say was…he looked gooood.

We continued to make small talk about the weather and my new plant obsession till the waitstaff sat us at our seats.

"As promised," he pulled out a horse on a keychain and passed it to me, "here is your horse."

"Oh great," I said, shaking with laughter. "Now I can't lose him!"

"Here, let me do it for you." He reached out to help when he saw me struggling to put him on my keys.

We kept talking and laughing about Sorry I Texted You When I was Drunk until the waiter came to ask for our order.

"Oh, I haven't even looked yet. Can I get a minute, please?" I replied to the waiter while tossing Joe a smile. I looked down. "What do you suggest?" I asked Joe.

"Well, it depends," he stated flirtatiously. "Do you eat meat? Can you handle spice?"

"I love chicken and of course I can handle spice," I flirted back.

"Alright. But this is really spicy, even for me," he said cautiously, with a glint of a dare in his eyes.

"Please," I retorted. "Cayenne pepper is my favourite spice."

The confidence of the cayenne pepper and my power suit must have convinced him.

"Okay," he said. "There are several spicy options: the Chicken Jaffna or Chicken vindaloo. There's also a spicy vegetable curry." He looked up at me with a sneaky smile tugging at the corners of his mouth, "If you chicken out, there's always the rice."

I gave him what I assumed was an assured but cute look.

"I'll take the chicken vindaloo," I said definitively.

"Miss, that is really spicy," the waiter warned me.

"I can handle it," I toss back. "Plus, I'm paying since it's the reward for finding my horse."

"If you can survive the chicken vindaloo, it'll be my treat," Joe ventured.

"Alright. Bet."

We shook hands.

The waiter rolled his eyes.

While we waited for the food, we talked more about ourselves. He told me about his childhood in the Caribbean to which I asked innocent questions about his family there, the education and traditions and acted surprised when he told me about his aunt's wedding at "the most beautiful venue." But nothing compared to when he commented on my heels.

"You know, not a lot of girls wear heels on the first date anymore. They always want to see how tall I am first."

"How bizarre?" I responded from behind my glass. *Thank you, Jess.*

The food came and I surprised everyone by eating the entire plate. Thankfully, a darkly lit restaurant provided the perfect cover for secret affairs, poor fashion choices, bloated bellies, and watery eyes.

A few hours later, we made our way back to his place for some more wine. Since the night was warm we decided to walk the fifteen minutes to his house from the station all the while I was beginning to feel a little less confident in my eating ability as my stomach felt like I had swallowed a lit match. It must have been the rice.

Once at his place, he poured me a glass of sparkling white wine and suggested we go into the living room. In the corner he had a guitar and a stack of vinyl next to a vintage record player. My stomach gurgled.

"Still hungry?"
"Always," I laughed nervously.

He chuckled while I sent a quick prayer to the universe that the sparkling wine would put out the fire in my belly. Trying to put as much space as possible between him and my unsettled stomach, I moved across the living room and pointed to the guitar.

"Do you play or is it just here to impress the girls?" I asked, trying to continue my flirting. He went over to it.

"It's just here to impress the girls," he said.
"Does it work?"

He began to play one of those melodies you'd know from the radio but can't quite name while I listened and admired his skill. Holding my wine, I wandered over to the stack of vinyls and appreciated the assorted album collection; Bon Iver, Josh Groban, Whitney Houston, Queen, Guns n' Roses, Bonnie Taylor, Metallica, David Bowie, U2, Dolly Parton, and a couple names I didn't recognise but whose faces looked familiar.

gurgle

Hurriedly, I sipped my wine.

When he finished playing, we sat on the couch and talked more about our likes, interests, and passions. I didn't have to worry about awkward silences because my stomach filled in the gaps. He asked if I wanted a snack and then brought out bread, brie, and hummus.

I nibbled on the pita bread and brie as he told me about his favourite movie; Fast and Furious.
"Have you ever seen it?"
"Actually, no, I haven't."
"Well, you are not allowed to leave here until you have," he said with a wink.
"Alright." I smiled up at him.

double gurgle

About twenty minutes and a few make-out sessions into watching the movie my stomach situation was getting desperate. Now was the perfect opportunity to get to the bathroom. The movie was loud, and he was absorbed in it...well, enough for this anyway.

I politely asked where the toilet was, and he directed me to the door right between the kitchen and the living room. I sat up, straightened my shirt, gave him a sweet smile, and sauntered off to the toilet. Once inside, I speedily unbuttoned my trousers. My poor bloated stomach made it so I could barely see my toes. I sat down.

Okay, I just need to release a little bit of air.

I pressed on my tummy in the hopes of doing a small, ladylike burp. But what came out the opposite end can only be described as a trumpet's rallying war cry that echoed around the delicate porcelain walls.

Thank God for loud action scenes.

But, whatever, it had worked, and my stomach didn't hurt as much. I finished my business, pulled up my trousers, washed my hands and went out the door.

The movie was paused.

The room was silent.

I looked in his horrified eyes...

...damn these thin London walls.

++

That Wednesday the girls could do nothing but laugh at my expense.

"I then had to sit there for another 2 hours and finish the damn movie," I cried out pathetically, which made the girls laugh even more.

"Have you heard from him since?" Chanel asked while wiping away tears of laughter.

"No," I replied sadly.

Jess cut in, with the double standard argument, "Men

fart all the time! If he couldn't handle a single fart…."

"Girl," Riley said, struggling for breath, "that was the whole damn brass band!"

***

***

Every embarrassing moment is a great story for later.

***

VIII
A Thousand Years Later

Wine Pairing: An expired warm white wine from the box

***

---

*Ring 12:52 (Jonas)

I've been sat here for the past two hours and this stupid campaign just refuses to look good. What if I try this colour? Ugh no matter whatever I changed it to it just looks so bad. I dropped my head and massaged my temples.

---

*Ring 12:53 (Jonas)

It's always tough to refocus after a fun weekend with the girls.

---

*Ring 12:54 (Jonas)

The Mondays are a strange feeling. This one isn't so bad, I just can't focus. I adjust my blue light glasses.

---

*Ring 12:55 (Jonas)

I picked up the phone.

"Jonas!" I barked into the speaker, "What do you want? I'm at work."

"Hey sis, are you free?" My brother's carefree voice irritated me further.

Really, you're the king of the obvious.

"I have exactly four minutes before my boss comes back from lunch," I said, taking a calming breath. "What's up? Is everything okay?"

Jonas went quiet for a moment. The WhatsApp reconnected sound dinged in my ear.

"...now...thing...mum...years...lat...is that fine?" was all I could make out.

"Sorry, Jonas, you cut out for a second. Is everything okay?" I asked, starting to think that something might be wrong at home. "Are mum and dad alright? Did something happen?"

"No yeah, everything is fine," he said nonchalantly, as if calling repeatedly on a Monday afternoon was a normal thing and not meant to induce a streak of fear in children who don't live in their home country. "I was wondering if you could help me with something." He paused again and I could hear him munching on something through the phone as I breathed a small sigh of relief. He swallowed and then continued, "My friend from work is moving to London for a few years and doesn't know a lot of people there. I was thinking maybe you could show him around if that's fine with you?"

"Yeah, sure," I said, starting to refocus my attention on my screen. "I could always use new friends."

"Great. I'll give him your number and he'll message you."

"Sure," I said, suddenly getting an idea for the campaign. "I have to go. Who is it?"

"His name is Josh Carter."

"Cool. I'll talk to you later."

A few hours after that, when I had finished with the campaign, I became curious about my brother's request. I opened up social media, ignored the idea of looking at Rex's profile and searched 'Josh Carter' under my brother's friends. Two people popped up. I really hoped he was the guy with the concert profile picture and not the shirtless guy with the tiger.

The rest of the work week went fine. We got the campaign perfected and approved with no trouble, except for a few tears and several sleepless nights. The girls and I went for our weekly catchup dinner on Wednesday where our activity of the night was to watch Chanel and a beautiful stranger hitting it off. Thursday, I gave my number to the cute guy at the table next to me during lunch, who never messaged me- which was fine as I'd changed my number last year, and had clearly given him the old one. That weekend, the girls and I, except Chanel who was on a second date with the beautiful gentleman, went to a house party being thrown by the guy that Riley was seeing. By Sunday I had completely forgotten about my talk with my brother.

Once again I was sat at my desk on a Monday morning, looking at Pinterest, trying to come up with a theme for a client's advertisement launch in a month, when I felt my phone buzz in my pocket.

Yes! I knew the cute guy from the lunch place was having phone problems and would message eventually.

11:47 Unsaved number: Hey Em, it's Josh, Jonas's friend. He gave me your number last week. I've just moved into my new flat in Shoreditch so I haven't had a chance to message you. How are you?

Damn. The cute guy from lunch is clearly still having problems contacting me with my old number. It doesn't seem to be the shirtless tiger guy. At least, this profile picture isn't the same.

11:58 Em: Hi Josh. It's nice to meet you. I'm doing well, thanks. Shoreditch is a nice area. Welcome to London!

Oh well. My lunch break is in an hour; maybe I can try that place again. I'll make sure it's the right number this time.

A couple of Saturday's later the girls and I were having our monthly brunch in a new restaurant that Chanel had recommended where you can order champagne with the press of a button. Chanel was in the middle of telling us why she was debating breaking things off with the handsome man.

"But I thought things were going well with him," I said as I topped off Riley's champagne glass.

"Yeah, but he never texts me first during the day. I feel like I am constantly initiating the conversation and setting up when we will actually meet," She took a drink. "He only ever texts in response or after eight."

"Rule eighteen: if they initiate texting after 22:30 five times within the first four weeks, then they're a clown," Riley said. "Besides we know he doesn't work shifts."

"It's been a week and he's already messaged four times after nine. It isn't exactly the rule but it is still clown behaviour," Chanel said dejectedly.

"Aw Chanel." I reached out to give her a hug. "It's okay. You know what you need to do."

"Bin. Him," we said in unison with our glasses raised. "To the FNC list!"

As the handsome man disappeared into the Fuck No Clowns list, we continued our night. Riley was stressed about her potential promotion at work, as her caseloads had increased in the past two months but was proud about her making and devouring a whole red velvet cake in one sitting. For Jess, it was approaching the busiest part of the term but she was looking into a holiday with her boyfriend to celebrate their anniversary. Chanel was still searching for the perfect place to open a second coffee shop in East London.

We ordered lots of different starters to share amongst us while we waited for our main courses to arrive. Anytime we got thirsty we pressed the magical champagne button. As we waited for our next round, I mentioned my most recent family call.

"Oh yes, Em, how is your brother aka my future husband?" Riley turned to me with a giggle. "Still single? Ask about me much?"

No, he didn't ask about you, but I'm working on it. Our future plan to be sisters-in-law is still intact," I laughed as our drinks arrived. "Actually, he asked me about his friend Josh." They looked at me confused as I began to explain, "A couple weeks ago Jonas asked me to befriend one of his co-workers who recently relocated to London. His name is Josh. He seems nice."

"Em! Have you been talking to a boy for a whole week without telling us about it?" Riley cried out.

"No, no, no. I'm only meeting him as a friend. Lovely guy but he's far too young both literally and mentally. He still likes his champagne with lemonade."

We all laughed at memories of our younger days.

"But if you have any nice single younger girlfriends, let me know and I'll set it up for her. He seems fun and we could always use more guy friends on the man panel."

The following work week flew by in a flurry of deadlines and meetings. I was looking forward to a slow and restful weekend. That Saturday morning found me wrapped up in multiple blankets on my living room couch. We'd had a cold turn the last three days and, as my heater was still broken, being inside my flat felt like being trapped in an ice cube. Luckily, I was supposed to be going on a cute date to the National Portrait Museum with a sweet new match later that day. As the tickets to the museum were free, it would be cheaper and quicker than getting my heating fixed.

*ding

> 09:03 Josh: Hey, do you want to go for a drink later? There's a pub called The Silver Horseshoe in Shoreditch that I really want to try.
> 09:31 Em: Sure. What about after 4?
> 09:31 Josh: Great. I'll see you there.

Good, another couple hours of heating.

My date was lovely. In the morning, we visited the museum and then went to get ramen afterwards. When it was time for me to meet up with Josh, I said my goodbyes, and we both agreed to go on another date later that week.

I got to Shoreditch around 15:55. Turning left from the station, I made my way towards The Silver Horseshoe on Quaker Way and prayed to the universe that the pub would be warm and cozy.

It wasn't.

The place was a bit drab. It looked like time had stopped inside, with the people unknowingly trapped in. The decor hung off the walls in tears and shreds. The lamps dropped disgusting yellow light that somehow made the water more tasteless. Looking back outside the dusty windows you could see even the horseshoe on the sign was hanging upside down.

I took a picture and sent it to our group chat.

Get the Wine

16:02 Em: And this is how I die.

Twelve minutes later, Josh still hadn't shown up. As my phone was at seventeen percent, I looked around for somewhere to plug it in.

Not seeing any outlets, I asked the barman if there was somewhere I could charge my phone. The aged man looked at me and told me to wait a second so he could ask the manager, then proceeded to continue staring at the taps. Turning away slowly, I took a seat near the door by a window that overlooked the street. I kept glancing over curiously but the barman hadn't moved from his spot behind the bar. Eight minutes later with my phone at ten percent there was still no Josh, no response to my "I'm here" message, and worst of all, no manager.

This is fine. *nine percent.

Outside, the light grey clouds gathered to cover the blue sky and the weatherman's prediction of drizzle came true- if you can call one or two drops drizzling.

Finally, twenty-five minutes after I had gotten to the bar, the manager emerged from the back eating a wilted sandwich. Three minutes after that, the barman, seeming to remember I had asked a question, pointed the manager in my direction. Since he still was not there, I texted Josh that my phone was charging and where I was sitting.

I was not sure how late Josh was officially but what felt like an eternity after my phone had been taken, he finally walked through the door. He was tall with jet black curly hair, and brown eyes behind round glasses. He looked around twice before seeing me and slowly made his way over to where I was sitting.

"Sorry I'm late," he said to me in a monotone voice. "I got stuck in the rain."

"Oh," I said and looked outside at the semi-dry pavement. "I hope you don't get sick."

"Yes."

He sat down without saying another word.

Silence; he stared at me expectantly.

Silence; I turned to the window to escape the constant stare.

Silence; even looking out the window, I could feel my face flushing from his gaze.

What is he expecting me to keep up the conversation?

"Um...do you want to get a drink?" I asked cautiously, trying to break the awkwardness.

"Yes," was the monosyllabic response.

"Okay…" I turned to look at the bar. "Um...what kind of drink do you want? They have lots."

"I don't mind. Whatever you have."

"Do you like gin?"

"Yes."

Wow, really, giving me so much help here…

Standing up, I said, "Great. I'll get us two gin and tonics."

"Okay," he said, folding his hands on the table.

Hurriedly, I went up to the bar to order our drinks. *Maybe he's just nervous.* The barman slowly made our drinks. *Wait, why would he be nervous? God I hope these drinks help.*

It didn't.

It only got worse.

With every sip, the situation got more and more awkward.

"So how do you like London so far?" I asked as I tried to get something out of him.

"It's nice," he said plainly.

I took a sip.

"Do you work far from here?" I asked again, hoping for more of a response.

"No."

"How long do you think you'll stay here?"

"I don't know."

I took another sip to give him the opportunity to ask a question. He didn't.

"So...why did you pick Shoreditch?" I asked, hoping that this would yield a longer response.

"It looked fun." was his longer yet still monotone response.

"Oh, what do you do for fun?"

"I walk."

"Oh cool. I like to walk. Walking is nice."

I drank deeply from my glass. *An unboiled kettle would have had more to say than this guy.*

We sat in silence for a few more minutes. At this point, I must have been in the pub for around fifty minutes, which at least thirty of which had been by myself. My phone was probably at 20% which might be enough to get me home. I didn't want to be rude, so I decided to nurse the drink for a bit. I thought that staying another fifteen minutes was enough time to then make up an excuse to leave. I could just about see his wristwatch under his sleeve and began the countdown. I put my glass down.

"So, what do you do for work?" I tried again.

"I.T."

"Cool. Do you like it?" I asked without curiosity.

"Not really."

I took a big sip.

"What kind of job would you rather do?" I asked.

"Music."

"Oh. That's interesting. Why don't you do that?" I asked, genuinely curious this time.

"I need money," he said without expression and a small shrug of his shoulders.

I took another deep drink from my glass.

"Makes sense. Do you make music for fun?"

"No."

"Oh…."

I looked at his wristwatch. It had only been five minutes and I only had a sip left.

Damn it.

I finished the drink.

Instantaneously, the barman came around to collect my empty glass.

"Would you like anything else?" he asked me in his snail-paced voice.

"Yeah, can we get two more of these?" Josh butted in, pointing at his partially full drink. I turned to him shocked. *First of all, rude to order for me without asking, but of course now he decides to speak up.* I smiled politely. *Damn you, Jonas.*

With speed that I had not thought possible of him, the barman left to get us our new drinks. *Alright, if this guy isn't going to say anything, I guess it's embarrassing story time…*

For ten minutes I talked about the time my jeans ripped in the middle of the night club back home and how the boy I had a crush on pointed and laughed at me. When he didn't laugh or come in with his own embarrassing story, I told him about the time I fell flat on my face in front of my then boyfriend's parents and mooned them. Again, no response to my hilarity.

I had drained my second gin and tonic between my stories. The moment I finished my drink I stood up, not even daring to put the empty glass on the table.

"I'm going to go to the toilet," I announced as I took said empty glass to the bar.

"Hi, could I please get the bill for the table by the window and my phone please?" I said quickly and quietly. "I'm in a bit of a rush."

It took five minutes for the barman to bring me my bill and what felt like forever to get the phone. I looked back at Josh. He was just staring at the seat that I had been previously occupying.

There's no way this guy can be on our man panel.

Finally, I had my phone and my change. I headed back to the table to make my excuses.

"Hey, it's been so nice getting to talk to you, but I have to head home and get ready for tomorrow. I've already paid the bill, so you don't have to worry about rushing out of here. Enjoy the rest of your drink and I'll see you around some time." I moved towards the door.

The chair scraping on the floor caused me to look around- Josh had stood up.

"Okay."

"No. Really, it's fine," I said encouragingly. "Finish your drink. I insist."

"That's okay. I don't really like it anyway."

"Oh. Okay. Well, bye." I turned and I walked out the door. A few seconds later, I heard him walking behind me.

"Are you going to the station as well?" I asked, "Don't you live nearby?"

"Yeah. I want to make sure you get home okay."

My God. NO! Please no. It's five o'clock; the light is still out. There is no need. My God. No.

"Thanks. It's okay though," I said to him.
He continued to walk next to me in silence.

Thank God the station is only two minutes away.

When we got to the station, I turned around to say goodbye except he walked past me and through the barrier.

DEAR LORD NO.

"Josh, really, it's okay. You should stay. I know you're trying to be a good friend. But you don't need to. You live here. You don't need to waste an hour going there and back."

"No. I like the tube."

I give up. Accepting the fact it was going to be a boring ride, I made my way through the barrier.

We sat in silence on the train for what was the longest train ride home. He didn't look at me and I stared out the window into the bleakness as I refused to continue to try and fill the silence. Never before had I noticed how loud the rails were.

An eternity and one thousand years later we arrived at my station. I sprang up.

"Thank you for making sure I got here alright," I said as I jumped out of the carriage. "Enjoy your ride back home." Josh stood up, got off before the doors, but instead of going to the other side of the other platform, he strolled in silence towards the exit.

I sighed.

In more silence, we made our way up. I stopped before the barriers and said bluntly, "Really, this was too much. You've done enough for me already. It'll be late when you get home. I'm okay. Have a good tube ride back."

He then proceeded, without emotion or expression and in complete seriousness, to suggest, "Or we could go to yours and drink some wine. I know this nice organic brand that doesn't give you hangovers."

And that, ladies and gentleman, is when I realised that I had just been on a date.

***

***

We're so lucky today that there are so many different ways that you can meet people: dating apps, in pubs, through an introduction, or through random happenstance.

You just never know how you will meet someone or when a person might become more than just a face you pass by regularly.

***

IX

Number 74

Wine Pairing: Casa De Vila Verde 2019

***

Girl Get the Wine

07:22 Jess: ITS WINTER WONDERLAND
DAYYYYYYYYYY
07:22 Jess: What time are we meeting?
09:08 Chanel: A little excited there Jess?
09:08 Jess: ITS WINTER WONDERLAND DAYYYYY
09:12 Em: YES! Let's meet at 11 at the normal spot.
10:50 Chanel: I'm in front of the National Portrait Museum by the steps. Where are you?
10:53 Jess: I'm just getting off of the tube. I'll be there in a second.
11:00 Em: I'm walking from my stop to Riley's stop. We'll meet you in a couple minutes.

It was about two on a Saturday afternoon, and our fourth annual Christmas Fun Function. Ever since Jess, Riley, and I had been in London, we had chosen a day to go to as many Christmas markets around that we could. It started out innocently with us looking for Christmas presents for our friends and family back home and finding the best hot chocolate for us. After a couple of years, we had mapped out the perfect day to spend together before the Christmas rush.

The first thing we did was go over to the small market in front of the National Portrait Museum in Trafalgar Square for crepes and coffee. Then, we walked to Leicester Square to check out the smaller vendor shops and burn off the crepes. After a quick pit stop, we continued to walk throughout London looking at the Christmas trees, lights, and the different decorations that various store fronts had up. Sometime in the afternoon, we would arrive at Jess's favourite part of the day: Winter Wonderland in Hyde Park.

Usually we would go on the rides for a while before Jess would get motion sickness and volunteer to look after our bags in a tent with music and multiple cups of hot cider. A little while later Chanel would join her when it started getting really cold. As payment for coming with her on the rest of the rides, I would challenge Riley to participate in one of the game booths to try and win me a prize. Usually she would get something small but this year she won the jackpot.

"This reindeer is stupidly big," I said as I shifted the ginormous stuffed animal to my left side while we briefly met up with Jess and Chanel in the tent.

"At least you won something!" Jess said excitedly as she put her long brown hair up into a bun.

"Yeah, did you see that guy's face?" Chanel interjected. "He had been there trying to win that for his boyfriend for ten minutes before we got there. He looked really jealous."

"I should have given it to him," I complained, shifting it back to the right again.

"Nope. You wanted it." Riley laughed. "Come on let's go on more rides. Just leave it here for now."

When Riley had finally had her fill of roller coasters and rides, we met up with the others at the pavilion for a drink and a second lunch of bratwurst and halloumi fries. Every year there was a different band that played covers of popular songs and their own special variation of *Sweet Caroline* which was what this year's band was playing as we came in. I plopped the stuffed reindeer down on the seat next to me.

"You stay there Mr Reindeer."

"No! He can't be a 'Mr Reindeer.' That's so unoriginal." Riley said sarcastically.

"Why don't you name him Mr Darcy?" Jess suggested giving him a pat on the head.

"Yeah, everyone should have a Mr Darcy in their life," Chanel said.

We sat there for another few hours drinking our piping hot mulled wine while making holiday plans for next summer's girls trip, talking about Chanel's chances of opening a coffee booth the following year, Riley's latest one-night stand, analysing Jess's relationship with Will as only single females can, and mulling over New Year's resolutions that we could maintain the pretence of keeping at least till the end of February.

Soon, the sun had gone down and the crowds had started to double. I pulled my white coat trimmed with faux fur closer around me. I hadn't been feeling particularly well for the past two days and my idea to self-medicate with mulled wine wasn't curing me.

"Girls, I think I have to call it a night and take Mr Darcy to his new home."

"I was just about to ask you for the keys to yours," Riley said to me. "I'm exhausted. Let's head back." She drained the last of her lukewarm wine. "But you're carrying Mr Darcy."

Thirty minutes later we were finally out of the park and twenty minutes after that we were finally almost home. At the top of my street, I gave up my duty of care and dragged Mr Darcy on the pavement behind me.

"Whoa there, did you steal Santa's ride?" a cheeky voice joked behind me. I whipped around to see the local neighbourhood hottie walking behind us.

"There were no Ubers available. What else was I supposed to do?" I joked as he caught up with us, graciously picked Mr Darcy up off the ground, and fell into step with us. "You know you are aiding and abetting an outright burglary…theft…kidnapping...reindeer-napping…. right now?" I said playfully as he swung Mr Darcy over his strong shoulders.

"Oh shoot. I heard that you can do some hard time on the naughty list for aiding and abetting a reindeer-napping. I guess he had better not catch us," he said as he put Mr Darcy down on my doorstep.

"Thanks Alex," I gave him my most charming smile. "See you later. Keep an eye out for any red flashing lights in the sky. Don't want to get caught."

"With legs like these," he said, gesturing down, "I'll be able to run away from the North Pole Reindeer Crime Unit."

Riley looked at me like I was dumb while I laughed and watched Alex walk away, leaving us with a fine view of his assets.

"Um...who was that?" Riley asked, intrigued by this mysterious neighbourhood hottie.

"Alex?" I asked casually as I unlocked the door and juggled Mr Darcy on my other side. "Oh, he lives somewhere on the street. We run past each other occasionally. He's nice."

Walking in, Riley burst out laughing. "You run?"

"Okay, so I'm walking and he's running and sometimes I'm just sitting on the stoop while he's running. You know, running."

Taking a seat on my couch next to Mr Darcy while I went to the kitchen to grab us some water, Riley asked, "How often do you guys text?"

"We don't," I called from the kitchen.

"What? With chemistry like that, you guys never text?"

"I don't have his number."

"WHAT?"

"I'm too nervous and he's never asked."

"Em, come on, he clearly likes you."

"I know but…"

"No buts, just do it yourself. What is the worst that can happen? He says no? Not a big deal," Riley argued.

"Fine, fine, okay. The next time I see him, I'm getting his number," I declared with confidence. I handed her the glass.

"Good," Riley said, standing up. "Now let's find Mr Darcy a stall for the night. We can't let the NPRCU spot him so easily."

It wasn't till a week later that I saw Alex again. Sometime back in late November, Jess and I thought it would be a great idea to sign up for swimming classes, which - according to the fascinating article we read - was a much better form of exercise compared to walking. Both of us had gotten our free first month passes and had used them all of three times. That Sunday was going to be the fourth hole in the card and the first punch in three weeks. Around forty minutes before class was to start, I headed to the corner tube station to make it there on time. I was a few houses away from the end of the street when I saw Alex walking towards me and gave him a big smile.

"Well, aren't you up early this morning." he said, looking me up and down. "You look active. Where are you going?"

"Ha, thanks. I'm just going to swim practice," I said.

"No way. Where do you swim? I love swimming." He stopped in front of me.

Well that explains his shoulders. Smiling at him, I adjusted my yellow swim bag before answering, "Not far from here. Glacier Centre in Waterloo."

"Me too. That's a great pool," he said excitedly. "Funny, I've never seen you there." He paused as I looked down, trying not to be suspicious. "What time do you go? I'm usually there before work."

"Oh, darn, I always go after work or on the weekends,"

I said as if I went to the pool regularly.

"And the weekends?" he said, clearly impressed. "Alright, you're making me think that I should start going on the weekends." He gave me a flirtatious wink. "Well, have a good practice. I'll see you around. Bye." He smiled again and continued walking.

As he walked further away from me, I whispered words of encouragement to myself. *Come on Em. You can do this. Just ask for his number. What's the worst that could happen? It's not like he lives right next to me. Just do it.*

"ALEX, CAN I HAVE YOUR NUMBER?" I yelled to him as a big London bus rolled past us.

"Sorry, what did you say?" He stopped and looked back at me with a twinkle in his eye. "I didn't catch that with the bus going by."

"CAN I GET YOUR NUMBER?" I shouted again as whistles of encouragement came from the group passing on the other side of the street.

"Oh, you want my number," he said, grinning. "Alright. We can do that."

I was late to practice but it was worth it.

A couple Wednesdays later, Jess and I met at the leisure centre to cancel our classes.

"Aw, Em. You didn't have to dress up for us," Jess said as she took in my leather trousers and lace bodysuit covered by a black blazer. "I mean, you look great. But we're just getting our weekly dinner, not going to the Oscars," she joked, and opened the door to the leisure centre.

"Ha," I responded as I handed Jess my card to pass on to the front desk, "very funny. Actually, I'm going on a date at half seven so I'm just coming for appetizers and a drink."

"Oh, with Alex?" she asked, leaning on the side of the front desk, while the attendee was handling our membership termination.

"Yeah. I just found out he lives two doors down from me. I can't believe it. On my walk, yesterday, I passed his flat and thought about how I could literally leave at 19:30 from mine and still not be late."

Even the girl behind the counter laughed at that one.

Five minutes later, we could hear Riley laughing as we opened the door to our favourite pub in Waterloo. They'd taken a seat at our normal table at the far side of the pub away from the door and everyone else. As we walked towards them, we caught a tidbit of the story that Chanel was telling that had Riley in uproars, "Then I realised it was a cat!"

"What happened?" I asked while taking the seat next to Riley.

"Oh. My. God. I can't breathe," Riley gasped out.

"Long story short, this young family walked in. I couldn't hear them until they were at the register but while the mums were talking and planning their weekend meet up, one of the little girls just looked up at her mum and went, 'Mummy, we can't go that day. It's Kevin's birthday.' to which the mum replied, 'Honey, Kevin doesn't know when his birthday is. It will be okay.' Turns out Kevin was the cat."

"THE CAT!" Riley gasped out between her fits of laughter.

"That's hilarious," Jess giggled as she took the menus Chanel offered and passed them to me.

One beer, half a bowl of chips, a cheeseburger, and three slices of the table's meat lover pizza later, I emerged from the pub with just enough time to get to my date. All those swim practices had really built up my appetite.

At precisely 19:30 I knocked on number 74.

The door swung open to a warm white light pouring into the night. Alex stood framed in the doorway, his black hair a bit tousled, clean-shaven, in a blue button down denim shirt with grey jeans. He adjusted his Clark Kent glasses.

"Hi Em. Right on time. Did you find your way alright?" he smiled cheekily.

I just laughed. "Luckily, I can count the twenty steps from my house to yours."

He laughed and moved aside to let me in and offered to take my coat. On the rack behind him, there was a dog lead.

"Oh, do you have a dog or some sort of fetish?" I asked, looking at him mischievously.
He burst out laughing, "No, no. I have a pet fish. The lead is for my job."

"What? As a dominatrix?"

"Almost. I'm a vet," he laughed out loud.

"Cool. Cool. Cool. Have you ever dognapped for someone before?" I asked, looking around innocently.

"Ha, no."

"Sure. Okay. I believe you. But that lead is still pretty suspicious if you ask me. And I know someone who would pay a pretty penny for a cute Samoyed," I winked at him.

"I'll keep that in mind," he laughed again, not taking my semi-serious proposal seriously. He gestured toward the living room area.

The layout of the flat was similar to mine but his heating worked a lot better. Down the hallway, you could see the ensuite in the back. The kitchen was along the left side of the front and opened up into the dining area which made for a bigger looking space. Tucked away in the corners of the rooms and hall were big vases of painted clouds, pointed mountains with peachy- orange-coloured fish that filled the ponds and baskets that the villagers were carrying on their heads as they walked home. Along the walls of the living room area, he had his fish tank, a TV, and a traditional Chinese tapestry.

I went over to the tapestry. It hung in three pieces above the dining table. In the middle were the blue and green of the rounded, thin mountains that were so different to the ones I had known all my life. On the right, you could see the clouds rolling in over the blue and red trees that stood nearly as tall as the mountains. Compared to this tapestry, the mountains on the vases looked like foothills. Finally, on the left, tiny rivers trickled off the sides of the cliffs into mystical ponds filled with golden fish swimming around. On each piece, lines of Chinese writing were printed in neat rows. It set the perfect backdrop for our date.

"I love it," I said in awe. "Where is this?"

"It's from Beijing. I go to China every three years to visit family. Most of my family is in Hong Kong but a couple of trips ago I decided to do a big tour of China with my Dad. He got this for me because I was just starting out and didn't have anything to hang in my first flat. He thought this would be nice."

"Oh I love that. I think it's important to live in different parts of the world," I said, thinking back on my own experience. "When did your dad move here? Or is he still in Hong Kong?"

"He moved here twenty years ago with my Mum and me. I was actually born in Hong Kong. My Mum is English and met my Dad while she was on a holiday with some friends when she was in her twenties. They were at an airport when my Mum and her friends got into a mix-up at the baggage claim and my Dad, who was – is – a pilot, helped them out because he's fluent in English, Spanish, Chinese, and Japanese. It was love at first sight." Alex paused, pushed aside his hair and continued, "My Mum moved to China six months later to be with him and taught English at a local school.

"A few years later, they were married, a few years after that, they had me. We lived in Hong Kong till I was about eight. When my English Grandfather got really sick, they decided to move to England. We've been here ever since." He started walking towards his kitchen. "I've just got pasta on the hob." I followed him. "What about you?" he asked. "What's your story?"

In the kitchen, he offered me a small glass of wine from his impressive wine shelf, which I accepted and drank slowly because I was trying to make room for this cheesy, heavy pasta. While I told him my story, he cooked with a towel over his shoulder.

Chanel was right, it is sexy to watch your date make your dinner.

Moving on from our childhood homes, we talked about normal things; where we had gone to Uni, how we'd decided on our respective careers, and our favourite type of crisps. You know, all the important things.

The dinner was amazing, but I couldn't eat as much as I wanted- I only managed two bowls. The one time I'd decided not to come hungry was the one time I wished I had been. After dinner, we cleared our plates, got another glass of wine and moved to the couch. We sat looking at each other, our knees touching as I animatedly talked about the most supportive place in the world is the girl's bathroom on a night out. However, I was rudely interrupted when he went for the kiss. It was a good kiss. It was that type of passionate kiss that you can't not fall into.

I mean, I'm literally two steps away from my bed. It's practically home anyway.

Around 02:00 in the morning, my stomach started growling. The pain in my abdomen had woken me up around 01:30 and I couldn't go back to sleep. I tried to stay still so that I wouldn't wake Alex, yet the familiar pressure on my stomach made me realise what was about to happen, but there was no way I was going to make the same mistake I made with Joe; especially when Alex's toilet door was right next to the bed. As the pain got more intense, I tried to lie as quietly as possible, while internally I tossed and turned over the idea of either risking it in the toilet next to his room or going home and stealing back in.

Screw this, I'm going home. What's the point of being so close to my own toilet and not using it for this emergency? There's no way he would realise that I'd gone out to use the bathroom. I'll be back in a few minutes, twenty minutes tops.

With the skill of a Russian spy, I stole out of bed, quietly dressed, tiptoed out of his flat and sprinted into the safety of my own bathroom. More than a few minutes later, I grabbed my keys and went back over to his flat.

With complete and utter dread, I realised that I couldn't get back in, as my dumb ass hadn't left the door open or taken his keys as I was in such a hurry. I was stood outside of his flat in the freezing early morning hours thinking over my options.

One: bang on his door and wake him up, but then I will have to explain what had happened, as I can't lie to save my life.

Two: send him a message and make a lame excuse about why I had to go home, which would insult him in the process.

Or three: never message or see him again and pray to the universe that he didn't remember me.

I meant to pick two, but somehow I ended up picking option three.

++

I know, I know, I didn't handle that well however I did eventually put on my big girl pants and apologise to him. I ran into him more than six months after this and told him everything; okay, the boy friendly version. We laughed about it and he agreed that what I had done was probably the best idea. We've seen each other on the street a few times since then. It's just gone back to how it was before. Except, he makes a lot more bathroom and ghost jokes now.

***

***

A topic for discussion at your next girls' philosophical debates;
is it easier to be the ghost or to be ghosted?

***

X
Business or Pleasure?

Wine Pairing: The forgotten empty wine bottle of red on the top shelf

***

I met Tyler Thompson at a work event. He was the CEO of a well-known razor company that was throwing their anniversary party in our hotel. It was the time of year when the months were slipping from June to July, with a lot more sunshine and a little less rain. His company had rented out the rooftop bar and the top floor just in case the weatherman had been mistaken.

While scouting out the best places for photos, I had seen an older attractive man around while I was taking photos of the setup process to post on Instagram. I was organising a trial shoot on the rooftop underneath the hanging ivy decorations we had just invested in. From that vantage point, you had a great view of London. To the right, you could see the river and the London Eye in the distance; to the left, buildings of grandeur and prestige. While I was trying to find the best way to get the whole view in a photo, the mysterious man in a suit and Carol, the event planner, passed me.

"...for the speech, I was thinking that it would start at half past eight over here. We would set up a microphone and speaker system a little way from the doorway so that people inside could see you as well," Carol was in the process of explaining to the silver fox with her.

"Yes. That sounds fine," he responded while looking me over.

"Excellent. Ah, here is Em," finished Carol, noticing him looking at me. "She is our PR and Social Media Manager.

Em, Mr Tyler Thompson. He is the CEO of the company. Sir, Miss Em Mahogany."

For a second, the world froze and his brilliant green eyes met mine.

"Nice to meet you, Miss Mahogany," he said in a baritone voice as his eyes smiled at me.

"You as well, sir. Em is fine," I replied, trying to sound professional and not overly excited.

"Please, call me Tyler."

"Alright, Tyler," I responded in what I hoped was a calm and collected tone. I couldn't hear myself very well as the butterflies were making quite a lot of racket in my stomach.

"If you would like to continue with me, I can show you the rest of the layout," Carol said, annoyed, while fiddling with her red glasses. She spun away from me. "Miss Mahogany has a meeting with Miss Stampson in a bit to discuss possible PR opportunities. Therefore if there is anything you would like to add please feel free to tell her to raise it with Miss Mahogany."

"Will you be attending the party tonight, Em?" Tyler interrupted Carol politely.

"Yeah, I have to take and post photos for the hotel's social media."

"Excellent. I will see you tonight."

The butterflies left my stomach region and flew north.

That night I wore my gold pantsuit with matching heels. My long hair was in a low bun with a few strands out to accentuate my high cheek bones. I was stationed by the dark green ivy decorations the whole night so, despite my efforts, I wasn't able to fashion an accidental run-in with Tyler again though he was in view often enough. However, at the end of the night, one of his assistants brought me his business card.

Once I got home, I returned Riley's missed call and we caught up on our days. She reported on the great date she had just been on with her current man of the hour, Julio, and I told her about Tyler. Together, we tried to figure out if Tyler meant to take me out on a date or for a business dinner.

"I don't know," Riley said, "but you should probably message him soon. Wait, send an email as messaging to his mobile is a bit unprofessional."

The next morning, he emailed back.

08:00 Friday, 28 June

Good Morning Em,

It was great to meet you last night. The function was lovely. It was a great turn out.

Regards, Tyler.

Damn, the business card was just for work, I thought to myself with bitter disappointment.

08:23 Friday, 28 June
Dear Mr. Thompson,

Yes. It was a wonderful turnout. I am glad to hear that you enjoyed the party and that our services were to your liking.

If you need anything again, please let me know.

Kind Regards, Em

Probably never hear from him again.

*ding

08:25 Friday, 28 June
Dear Em,

Yes, actually I do. I was wondering if you were able to have a dinner meeting later this week?

Regards, Tyler

Wait, is this a date? A business meeting? But who schedules a dinner business meeting with someone they just met? And we don't have any business in common. It isn't like we are equals in the work hierarchy. What would we have to talk about? So, it has to be a date. Right? I asked myself, the butterflies flying straight back into my stomach.

08:37 Friday, 28 June

Dear Tyler,

Yes. I can do that. I am free any time after work except on Wednesdays.

Kind regards, Em

I went to respond to my boss's latest email.
*ding

08:37 Friday, 28 June

Dear Em,

What about next Thursday at 18h00?
Regards, Tyler

How do I respond to something in a way that is professional-yet-nice, potentially-could-be-a-date?!

08:45 Friday, 28 June

Dear Tyler,

I look forward to it.

Kind regards, Em

08:45 Friday, 28 June

Dear Em,

Perfect, my assistant will send a message with all the details to the number in your email signature

Regards, Tyler

Damn, work.
Both the butterflies and I exited the email thread.

The rest of the day I tried to focus on the work in front of me but somehow kept returning to the email thread trying to figure out if this was a date or not.

*ding

16:30 Unsaved Number:
Dear Ms. Mahogany,
Please find the details for your evening with Mr Thompson
next Thursday.
Kind regards, Elizabeth

attached file

Sigh. Definitely work.

      That next Wednesday, we were all out at our favourite 'next week is payday' pub giving our weekly updates. When it was my turn, I asked their opinion on the Tyler situation.

"How the hell are you supposed to dress for a work meeting that could be a date?" Jess asked while grabbing a chip.

"I've been trying to figure it out all week. I have no idea," I complained. "I mean, it really sounds like it's just a business meeting. Maybe I should just wear what I wear to work but with some spice..."

Chanel nodded while eating her tacos. "You do dress well for work, but you can also make it a bit sexier. You know, unbutton a few top buttons in the washroom."

"Okay," I agreed. "Maybe a shirt dress with badass heels or something."

"You'll be fine," Jess said encouragingly while Chanel nodded enthusiastically next to her.

"Yeah, you're good in a business setting and usually pretty level-headed," Chanel added. "If you need to, just excuse yourself, and remember to breathe. Plus, you can always text one of us."

I nodded while chomping into my burger.

"Just remember to lock the bathroom door," she joked.

Riley almost choked on her cider.

The next morning, I pulled on a blue and white striped shirt dress, tied it at the waist with a black belt and tossed a thin, navy blue blazer over my shoulders. To pull the look together, I added some cheap gold jewellery, paired it with nude heels and donned an oversized light beige trench coat for the office.

The work day was uneventful. 16:45 rolled around and I started to map out how I was going to get to the restaurant as I sighed for the millionth time about how I didn't have a personal driver. Instead, I was going to have to take the Bakerloo line and a bus to get to this work date.

It was a romantic, little, family-owned Italian restaurant that had the most beautiful back garden. Strung across the open sky were fairy lights that highlighted the gorgeous patio and flower arrangements in a way that made it seem a bit dreamy. *Date, definitely,* I thought to myself as I was escorted to our seats, but I ordered a Coke just in case I was wrong. I didn't want to come across as unprofessional.

17:30 Unsaved Number:
Dear Ms Mahogany,
Mr Thompson would like me to tell you that he is stuck in a meeting. He will be at the restaurant in 20 minutes. He has instructed me to tell you that you should order an appetizer if you are hungry.
Kind regards, Elizabeth

Sweet; but also kind of weird for a possible work meeting.

I replied saying it was fine. However, I kept my figures crossed my phone battery would last till then. Even though I had charged it to 75% at work, it had been hovering around 30% since I had walked through the doors of the restaurant. If this was a work meeting and if he was any later, there was no way that we were going to be able to do work with my phone dead.

When I was a third of the way done with the fried calamari, he arrived. He was wearing a gorgeous blue suit with silver cufflinks that matched his hair. Giving me a nod, he slowed down as he was still on a phone call with what I assumed was work. After a few minutes, he took out his airpods, gave me a cheeky smile, and joined me at the table.

"What? No wine to go with your calamari? That's almost barbaric! Waiter," he turned around with his hand in the air, "Waiter, can we get a glass of Pinot Grigio for the pretty lady, please."

Ten minutes later, after he had asked about my last relationship and asked for any unique London dating stories while pouring me another glass of wine, I excused myself to the bathroom, double locked it, stuffed the blazer into my work bag and unbuttoned the top two buttons.

This is most definitely a date.

The next three months with Tyler passed by in a whirl of dinner dates, weekends along the Mediterranean, and adventures in the north of England to be with his young son. He went up north every second weekend and I sometimes joined as a way to get a mini-escape from London.

Though that was all fun, my favourite nights were the cosy evenings at home by his fireplace. He was a fantastic cook and loved to show off his skills, which was great as I loved to show off how much I could eat. He even cooked me seabass one time, which was definitely worth the wait. After dinner, we would watch his favourite rubbish British reality TV and it quickly became our thing.

For two such different lifestyles, we had a lot in common; we valued our friends and families, loved all-you-could-eat hotel breakfasts, didn't like to brag about our accomplishments, and we drank our coffee black. I took him to all my secret food places. Though they weren't his usual haunts, he seemed to appreciate them. He also got along well with the girls. Eventually, he started taking me to some of the places that showed who he was- more refined, elegant, and glossy. While they were different in aesthetic, price range, and typical customer type, he never made me feel out of place. But I didn't quite fit in with his crowd.

We had two big issues: one, my phone that was always dying in the middle of the day which made it hard to organise logistics when I didn't have a charger with me; and two, he got his pyjamas dry-cleaned while I was still sleeping in my ex's old t-shirt. Manageable issues, one of which I could fix with an easy shop at Primark and the other one, *well I'm due for an upgrade once my contract is done anyway.*

Get the Wine
19:07 Em: This feels like a dream.

"Girls, what should I get him for Christmas?" I asked while we were walking around Hyde Park. "I can't top whatever he's thinking about getting me."

"You don't need to." Jess exclaimed.

"He knows who he is dating," Chanel agreed.

"Yeah, he can afford those things," Riley added. "But you are what is unique in his life."

"Exactly," Chanel chimed, stretching her long legs against the park bench. "You are who he is choosing to date. What can you offer him that he wouldn't get elsewhere?"

The answer to my struggle was a London experience at the Aquarium, painting portraits of Jellyfish with a complimentary wine tasting. You know, weird but cool, right?

Okay, it was mainly weird. But we laughed a lot and his wall got some unique new art.

In comparison, he got me a handbag and a matching wallet. "I got you one more thing but I ordered it too late for the Christmas rush," he apologised. It didn't matter to me; the gifts were already too much.

We rang in the New Year together at an underground party in the East of London. We celebrated our budding love amongst the people I cared about the most. But the highlight of my night was seeing how Tyler was joking around with the girls. To this day, the word 'loofah' makes us burst out laughing.

Throughout January things were looking good. One time, he called me his girlfriend. It was on a voicemail and he was out with his friends. But still, he'd called me his girlfriend. At this point even Riley, who was the CEO and chairwoman of the FNC Red Flag Alert Association, gave him the green light. He told me that he had made exciting plans for Valentine's Day but he wouldn't tell me what they were as they were supposed to be a big surprise.

Then one day in early February he slipped into a coma…

…or at least that is what I assumed happened as I never heard from him again.

Over the next two weeks, I called and messaged his mobile, only to have it ring through to voicemails that he never returned. I even considered emailing or messaging Elizabeth but was told that could be weird by Riley. Chanel suggested going to all the different hospitals to check for him while Jess's suggestion of filing a missing person's report just seemed a bit too much.

Instead, I went with Riley's idea of calling him from her phone.

18:09 Phone Call Unsaved Number

"Tyler Thompson."
"Tyler?"
"Yes, who is this?"
"It's Em."
Silence
"Hello?"
*click

At least he kept his promise; I definitely was surprised on Valentine's day.

***

***

In case you were wondering what the Christmas present was- he got me a new phone. The card that came with it was as follows:

Dear Em,

This will probably not get to you before Christmas so I had to get you another quick gift. I can't wait to ring in the new year with you.
Hopefully this will improve our communication now that your phone won't always be dead.

Kind Regards,
Tyler

I mean it didn't but I don't think that was because of the phone.

***

XI
The Fire Exit

Wine Pairing: The Black Stump, Durif Shiraz

***

Oh great, I've become this driver's crazy work story to tell for the evening.

The tears fell from my eyes like the rain outside. There was no point in hiding it, I was sniffling with my head against the window of the tinted glass and my mascara was running. On the radio, Lewis Capaldi was crooning about heartache and unrequited love.

Sometimes, you just are the main character.

++

The night had started like any other date night. I finished work at 18:00 but arrived home after 19:00 due to an unexpected closure on the Circle Line. Anxious about making my 20:00 date, I jumped straight into the shower where I multitasked and mentally put together an outfit. Even though I was supposed to have returned it months ago, I still had Riley's dress that I had intended to wear for Valentine's day in my closet. It was a figure-hugging yet comfortable white wrap dress, that accentuated all the appropriate curves and angles of my body.

It would be a waste not to take it out. Shoot, I'm almost out of waterproof mascara. Should I risk it and just use the normal one? Whatever, it isn't like I'm going to cry. I threw on black heeled ankle boots and a cropped maroon blazer, and decided to keep on the gold jewellery I'd been wearing all day. After much debate, I tied my long blonde hair back in a sleek wrapped ponytail, after reapplying some dry shampoo which had been my saviour the whole day.

At 20:03 I hopped out of my Uber and walked into Bolton's, a popular restaurant frequented by the newest members of the financial services fraternity. Inside, you could see the modern design with black tables and matching chairs with white accents. The walls were a crème colour with a detailed leafy vineyard pattern that snaked upwards in no particular way, but which somehow made you feel outside. Behind the bar, there was an impressive array of gins, whiskeys, vodkas, and wines stacked on shelves that were lit up with a white light, allowing you to see every option. Aside from this, the place was darkly lit.

I was greeted at the door by a beautiful red haired and freckled hostess who took me to my seat three steps away. Two minutes later, my date arrived. He was wearing a yellow jumper with blue Argyll patterning on the front paired with black jeans and white Converse. Pictures didn't do him justice. In his photos, he was cute, but he was definitely the kind of man that you would show to your friends and say, 'Trust me, he looks better in real life.' Dreamy? Hell yes. Photogenic? I could teach him some tricks.

The hostess pointed him towards me as I waved to him. He gave me a charming smile as he approached.

"Em? Hi. I'm sorry I'm late. Have you been waiting a while?"

"Max, hello. No. I only got here a few minutes before you did. Take a seat."

He turned back to the hostess and asked hopefully, "Do you have any other tables available, so we don't need to sit next to the front door?"

"I'm sorry, sir, we are fully booked tonight. If anything becomes available, I will let you know," the hostess said, smiling apologetically.

Thanking her, Max sat down with a slightly disappointed look on his face.

"Honestly, I'm okay to sit next to the door if you are. I don't mind, but thank you for asking," I said a few moments later, when he glanced back at the door as another party walked in.

"It's alright. If you're happy then I'm happy."

I smiled back at him.

While we were waiting for our server to come to our table we talked about the weather, the turn of the season. In one of our first conversations he told me he was a pilot so I asked him about upcoming holidays and the destinations people might take.

"So many people go on holiday in April because of the school breaks," he explained, brushing his hair out of his face. "You wouldn't expect it. Whenever we fly in April, we're usually at 99% capacity. Those are the numbers we see during Christmas and the beginning of the Summer Holidays."

"That does surprise me," I said in all honesty, "but, I guess that makes sense; my family and I used to go away in April as well."

"Exactly. I actually have a busy rest of the month," he said looking back over his shoulder towards the windows as people walked by. He turned back to me with a dashing smile. "Tomorrow, I fly out to Italy and then come back the day after. The following week, I'm flying between China, Dubai, and Heathrow three times. Then at the end of the month I go to Rhodes. Have you ever been?"

"Yeah, once when I was younger," I said, playing with my bracelets.

"Can I get you anything?" the waiter asked with a notepad in hand and one hip thrust out. I took a sip of water, silently thanking him for the interruption. I didn't want to explain that one.

"Yeah," Max said, taking the lead. "Can I get a bottle of Merlot?"

"Of course. Will that be two glasses for you and the lady?"

"Yes, and can we have a refill on the bread and butter please?"

"I will bring that right out."

Max, you're speaking my language.

He was simply charming. Once the waiter had left, we continued talking about travel and our favourite cities. I got to show off my expert research on where to get the best cocktails in various cities. I made a note that, if we ran out of things to say, we could have talked about the people walking by, as he also seemed to be into my favourite past-time of people-watching. He looked up at everyone who walked by the front. When the door opened for the fifth time, I pulled my blazer close around me as a cool night wind blew in. Max clearly had the same idea as, even though we had been there for fifteen minutes, he was also still wearing his jacket.

"I see our server coming with the wine." Max stood up suddenly. "I'm going to the toilet really quickly. Please pour me a glass and I'll be right back," he said, giving me another flash of his charming smile and a glance towards the door. The chair squeaked on the tiled floor as he pushed it in.

"Okay. Sure," I replied as I watched him speed away.

The restaurant door continued to open and shut as more people came to claim their reservations. I pulled out my phone.

Get the Wine

20:22 Em: Things are going fine. He ordered a bottle of Merlot and asked the server to refill the bread bowl. This man gets me. He's in the toilet right now. Report back later.

20:25 Chanel: Have fun. If you need anything, just come to mine after. If you go to his, send us your location.

20:31 Em: <3 will do.

I put my phone away and proceed to partake in our shared interest of people-watching.

*Sip

I watched as a woman with a polka dot blouse reached for her purple velvet bag. *I wonder if she is also here for a date?*

*Sip

There must be a line in the toilet.

A young family left the restaurant with their crying baby.

*Sip

I look at my phone which has one new message from Josh.

Not now Josh. I'm on a date.

*Sip

The door opened again as more people entered.

Hmm, where is he?

The waiter comes up.

"Here is your bread and butter refill, ma'am. Can I get you anything else, an appetizer maybe?"

"Give us another minute, please. My date's still in the toilet."

"Yes, ma'am."

*Sip

This wine is really good.

A young couple in matching outfits walk past the door.

*Sip

I look down at my phone.

Twelve minutes. He'd better be quick or I'm going to finish it myself. I started to play with my bracelets.

I chewed on the table's bread for a change.

A bit later, I looked down at my phone again. *Fifteen minutes. But seriously, did he get stuck in there? Maybe the lock is broken?*

I kept munching my bread while I continued to wait and people-watch; somewhere outside a dog barked.

I hope he doesn't have food poisoning... Wait, he hasn't had anything yet.

It took another five minutes before a different thought entered my mind.

Did he leave? No, how could he just leave? It's not like this place is really big. I could have turned around at any second to see him walk out of the toilet. No, he must still be in there. There's no way.

I looked around. He was nowhere to be seen.

"Miss, are you ready to order now?" the waiter asked with a hint of impatience in his voice.

"I am, but my date has been gone for a while," I said looking back and trying to remain composed. "This is a bit of a strange question, but do you have another entrance to the restaurant? A smoking area? Are the toilets in another building?"

"No, ma'am, we don't have a smoking area and the toilets are just behind you."

"Are you sure?" I begged more than asked.

"Unfortunately, ma'am, this is the only door out of the restaurant. The only other way out would be through the toilet window or the fire escape by the kitchen."

"Oh," I replied as the realisation of what was happening hit me. "Thank you," I managed to whisper back as he turned and walked away.

Twenty minutes later I gave in. Not even girls fixing their makeup and complimenting each other's outfits in the washroom would be that long. I had long finished off the bottle of wine and was attempting to wave the server down for the check.

Before I could get anyone's attention, the lovely hostess approached me.

"Hi, another table further away from the door just opened up. Would you be interested in moving? I can show the gentleman to the new seat once he comes back."

"Um, actually, I was trying to get the bill. He seems to have left."

"Oh, okay let me get you the check," the hostess stopped to really look at me. "Wait, are you okay?"

"I'm not sure. I think I've just been ditched," I said in a voice that seemed small. Seeing her pitying face, I joked, "or he's just seen his girlfriend walk in and had to run away."

"What?" she said with a completely appalled look on her face.

"Yeah, I guess he either went out the fire exit or out through the toilet window."

"That's horrible! What a terrible man!"

"Honestly, I'm kind of in shock. This has never happened to me before. He didn't even have any of the wine. He went to the toilet just as it was coming out," I said, processing the event out loud.

"Oh, girl. No. We do not tolerate that kind of behaviour. It's a good thing he's gone. Don't even think about him for another second," the hostess said firmly. She looked at the door. No one seemed to be approaching so she pulled out his empty chair and sat down. I appreciated her kindness.

"Yeah, I know. It's just a bit harsh," I sniffled, "He could have just done the emergency call. It would have stung, but I wouldn't have been so confused." I sighed. "It just sucks because the last guy I was dating ghosted me after three months. Maybe it's just a me thing." I tried to force out a laugh but ended up looking down, as the tears were threatening to break the seal of my well-mascaraed dam.

"No. Listen to me. He was a disrespectful scumbag. Drop that trash right now. Go home, take a shower. Look in the mirror and say to yourself, 'You're a beautiful woman and you deserve someone who is kind, and respectful.'" She looked me dead in the face as she said, "Never allow someone to disrespect you. Never doubt your worth. And never cry over trash. Stand up and show them you have value."

I looked at her in awe.

"Thank you."

"Girl, we've all been there," she said as I reached down to get my wallet from the bag. "Don't worry about the wine and bread." She stood up, smoothed out skirt and went to re-tie her hair. "It's on the house. Just go see your friends and forget about these rude men."

I thanked her for her kindness and empowering words, put on my coat and opened that damn door.

Outside the rain was starting to fall from the heavens, which was the perfect ending to a rubbish evening. I called Chanel who could tell straight away from the quivering in my voice that something was wrong.

Phone Call Chanel: 21:05

"Hey, can I come over?"
"Yeah, of course. Are you okay?"
"I'll tell you when I'm there. Just have the wine ready."
"Okay. White or Red?"
"Both. I'll see you in 20."

My Uber pulled up to the curb while I was putting my phone away. Soaking wet, I got into his car. I struggled to maintain my composure as I greeted the driver and changed my drop off location to Chanel's flat. After I shared my live location with them the tears that had been threatening to fall began to roll down my face. On the radio, Lewis Capaldi was singing about heartache and unrequited love. I tried to cry like a lady in a Jane Austen book would but instead, I heaved and gasped as my mascara tears were racing like the raindrops on the other side of the tinted window.

"I met the love of my life on Lovematch. Your paths just haven't crossed yet. Download the app from the App Store today. What are you waiting for?" the radio crackled.

I burst out laughing while mascara tears still streamed down my face.

Looking up, I saw the Uber driver's shocked face. My only response was to give a small, teary smile and shrug.

The opening beats of the next song came on and Cindy Lauper's voice sang out about 'girls and fun.' I smiled into the window. Even though it was still raining outside, my tears had stopped.

++

"I can't believe he just left," said Chanel thirty minutes later. "What a clown move."

"Straight to the top of the FNC list!" proclaimed Jess while she poured me another draft of wine into my coffee mug.

"I know. But the worst thing wasn't even that he left," I mourned, biting into my kebab. "The worst thing was that my Uber rating went down."

***

***

Potential rule for our Rules List: always make sure you use waterproof mascara. You never know when you will cry.

***

XII
Networking

Wine Pairing: Tarantella Merlot 2018

***

There are a few rules that you need to follow when you start a new job. One: don't use the printer to print your own photos; two: don't use Karen's milk; and three: don't get a crush on the boss.

Well, I drink my coffee black anyway...

It was my second day and I had been warned by Karen in a company-wide email for the third time that no one should drink her milk and to stop eating her food with her name on it. Other than that, the new job was exciting. It was one of those larger PR companies that had a free snack bar and restocked the wine and beer fridge every Thursday. To say it was bigger than the little hotel was an understatement. Here, I was able to manage a team of six rather than one continuously hungover teenager. The team seemed nice, but as Riley had advised not to make friends with the people I was in charge of, I hadn't really befriended anyone.

I'd had some interesting conversations by the coffee machine that usually centred around the weather, tea orders, and weekend plans; but nothing that looked like it would lead to an immediate or lasting friendship.

That Thursday morning, coming back from the kitchenette, I was feeling particularly drained from being the new person. I slowly made my way back to my little side office as I tried not to spill the slightly over-poured coffee on my new company's carpet. The office wasn't super impressive, but I had my little cactus, Stan, and several photos of family and of our last girls' trip to Paris, so it felt more like mine.

We were working on a proposed campaign for a new car company from overseas. It was going to be seen across the world in massive arenas. No pressure. I had the team working on mock-up ideas for font sizes and reports on how they would look on different screens while I made my way through the different slogans we could use.

It was one of those days when the motivation was running late. Even the simplest of tasks felt like it took 110% of my brain power to process let alone complete. My feet were dragging across the floor like the minutes were inching past on the clock. Today was painful and I didn't even have the benefit of blaming a hangover. Putting down what was left of my coffee, I slouched in my chair and stared out the glass wall in hope that something would inspire me.

And then it walked in. If motivation was a 5'11 man in a grey suit with beautiful, dark brown hair slicked back, he walked in. I straightened up. No one who looked that refined could see me slouching and slacking off. I refocused my eyes on the computer screen and turned my attention to figuring out how to tell if he was looking at me without directly glancing up. I decided the best course of action was to go out to my team and check on how they were looking (doing, doing!). I stood up and knocked over Stan.

"Shit!" I yelled. Glasping my hand over my mouth. I looked up.

My team was looking right back at me confused.

And so was he with a serious look on his face.

I panicked and picked up the not-ringing phone.

"Hello? Yes, I'll be right there." I gently smoothed out my skirt and rushed quickly into a very important meeting in the ladies' room.

Get the Wine

09:42 Chanel: So what was his name?
09:45 Em: I don't know! He hasn't been back to the office in 4 days. Maybe he was just there for a business meeting. :(
09:47 Riley: Maybe
09:59 Jess: I can't do anything without a name, Em. I've already searched the website directory but they don't have many recent pictures.
10:06 Chanel: LOL
10:19 Riley: Why don't you just ask?
11:33 Em: Well, I will if he ever comes back!

It was crazy the lasting effect of this Motivation. Every morning I was early to work, dressed to the business nines with perfect hair and makeup, and my work was getting done (which was the most impressive out of all of this if you took into account how many minutes I wasted glancing up at the door waiting for him to come back).

Two wine fridge refills, a potential work friend, one completed project, ten perfect outfits, and zero sightings of Motivation later, I was beginning to believe that he was stuck in the same realm as Idris Elba waiting to get back to me.

One Tuesday, Riley, who had a rare day off, had come into the office to take me out for lunch and celebrate my new job. She arrived around 14:30 for a late lunch and was let up by security when I rang down to say I was running late.

"You're still not ready?" she said playfully as she walked into my little space. "Love the pictures." She took a seat.

I was busy finishing up the last bit of my proposal while simultaneously putting on my trench coat. "I know, I know. I'm sorry. I thought I would be ready. It's just this last sentence," I said, reaching over with half of the coat on and the other half hanging off me like I was a coat rack. I finished typing. "Okay. I'm good. Let's go." I closed my laptop and turned around to grab my purse.

"Oh he's fit," I heard Riley exclaim from behind me. WHOOSH. I whipped around.

MR. MOTIVATION?

I searched the room in hope till my eyes spotted where Riley was indicating. It wasn't Mr Motivation, but this guy was still very cute with dark curly hair that fell right above his eyes. From how he was perched on one of the other manager's desks, I couldn't tell how tall he was, but he seemed to be about as tall as Riley. He was wearing a black suit with a maroon tie. We must have been staring for quite a while because he waved to us.

"That must be the Head of Accounting, Felix Adams," I said to her as we nonchalantly waved back. "He's been on holiday since I started. I've never actually met him, but his automatic email response said that he would be back in the office today. Come on. Let's go. I'm hungry."

The next few weeks passed by at a normal pace. I wasn't constantly looking over my computer screen to see if Mr Motivation would walk in. My almost work friend and I solidified our friendship with salads from the downstairs cafe. The team and I sent in the car campaign and got celebratory drinks from the fridge afterwards. I was starting to feel more at home in this new position.

This could also be in part to the fact that I had started to bump into Felix Adams a few times a day. We always smiled and exchanged pleasantries but never really stopped to say anything else. But, I did notice that he usually took the same coffee break times that I did. So, I began to make sure to be there at the same time every day. Eventually, our shallow conversations gained more depth by talking about our favourite lunch spots.

"Besides the quality vending machine downstairs," he said one afternoon, "my favourite lunch place is this little kebab shop down the street."

"I'm sure it's great at three in the morning," I laughed loudly and then blew on my too hot coffee.

"I wouldn't know," he responded with a laugh in his eyes. "The place I usually go for that is on the opposite side of town."

"Ha." I burned my tongue.

"Trust me. I'll take you tomorrow," he said without noticing my wincing face.

"Ha okay," I replied.

"It's a date!" he exclaimed.

"Are you sure it isn't for work?"

"No," he said firmly. "It's a date."

I smiled all the way back to my desk.

However, the next day, Felix had to cancel on me because his 11:00 meeting was running over. But he promised to make it up to me by taking me out to dinner instead some time later that week. Not going to let his meeting ruin my lunch plans, I grabbed my things and headed out of the office. While I was waiting for the lift, I began planning out my afternoon in my head. On my phone, I opened my calendar and started scheduling the different tasks that needed to be completed before going home.

*bing

While the doors were opening, I finished up what I was doing and started to put my phone back in my purse. When I

looked up to walk in, there he was in front of me: all the
motivation I ever needed smiling back at me.

Get the Wine

11:24 Jess: WHAT'S HIS NAME!?
11:30 Em: Tomi Henricks

Turned out Tomi was the one of the big guys in the
finance department at the firm. Based on Jess's research, he had
graduated in a year that would make him about thirty-six. His
life seemed to be dedicated to work. All of his profiles were
public and all were either focused on the company or sharing
business related articles. Jess figured he was either too old to
have active social media accounts or he used a fake name.

Get the Wine

20:01 Riley: Or maybe he's secretly married
20:15 Em: Don't jinx it!
21:08 Jess: Or he's a ghost
21:32 Chanel: LOL but seriously, how was lunch with Felix?
21:34 Em: OH CRAP! FELIX! I have to reply to his message!

Somehow Tomi got my number. He didn't play games
and got straight to the point, asking me to get dinner with him
on the following Wednesday. It wasn't until after I had agreed
for Wednesday that I remembered I had rescheduled the date
with Felix for next Tuesday.

"Good luck girl," was all Riley could say.

That Sunday evening, I was the first to arrive at Jess's
'famous Hollywood movie night.' They were really just normal
movie nights but Chanel, Riley and I all got dressed up like we
were going to a premiere of something and Jess indulged us but

usually wore her pyjamas. To be honest, we all usually changed into our pyjamas soon after arriving as well.

*Ding

"Hey, Jess can you get my phone? It's on the couch I think. Is it Tomi or Felix?" I asked from the bedroom.

"Both," came her laugh from the living room.

"Haha, no really," I replied.

Jess burst out laughing.

"What's so funny?" asked Chanel as her and Riley walked through the door.

"Both of them texted her at legitimately the same time," Jess chuckled as she showed them the phone. They all laughed while Riley took it and walked into the room. "Look."

17:55 Felix: It was great to catch up at the water fountain earlier. I'm so excited for Tuesday.
17:55 Felix: I have something nice booked.

17:55 Tomi: I've been on a business trip all week. I've missed you a lot. Can't wait to see you on Wednesday. It's going to be fun.

"Never have I ever felt more like *The Bachelorette* than this moment," I proclaimed to them.

On Tuesday evening, I met Felix along the South Bank near the little open air book stand. He greeted me with flowers and a kiss on the cheek. Even in his casual outfit, he still looked good.

"I thought we could walk around for a bit before going to the restaurant," he suggested. "There are a few cool cocktail bars around here we could go to after. There's one that's set up like a cave."

"Just letting you know, the cave has my vote," I said, highly interested.

"Great," he smiled and took my arm. "That's my favourite anyway."

"Lucky you," I smiled back at him.

The evening was a pleasant experience. We laughed. We joked around a lot. We just got on really well. He even took part in my daydreams musings of what it would be like to be as fast as Usain Bolt on a daily basis and raced me down the street. After tripping over my heels, I lost our race. As penalty, I had to buy his first drink.

Dinner was at a local hotel restaurant followed by a few drinks in the cave. Around 01:00, Felix walked me to my station.

"This was great," he said, while running his hand through his curly hair. "Hopefully, I'll see you by the watering hole tomorrow…"

And then, we were kissing. Butterflies and a few missed trains later, I arrived home and sank into the comfort of my bed.

"Damn," I thought, "how is Tomi going to beat this?"

Get the Wine

13:07 Em: Girls, IDK what to do. I mean, I kissed Felix last night. It was such a great date. What should I do? Should I still go tonight?

13:18 Dee: So? Your point is...

13:36 Riley: I don't see your problem…

13:56 Jess: But Mr Motivation! You can't just not go!

14:00 Riley: ^^ do itttt

14:22 Chanel: Kiss Tomi and see who you have the best chemistry with.

14:35 Em: But what if one of them finds out?

14:51 Riley: You're single. Who cares?

16:12 Chanel: You're not hurting anyone. You'll regret it if you don't go.

Work the next day was long but I pulled myself together for my date with Mr Motivation. I was excited about Felix but when I saw Tomi walk through the office again, I knew I had to go on that date.

Tomi picked me up from my flat in his car a little after work. About forty minutes later we had parked near an open air market along the river in East London.

"I know you like food," he said to me. "So I'm going to get you all the food."

I giggled like a lady should but on the inside I was ready to eat all. The. Food.

For twenty minutes we went to several different booths and ordered an exquisite selection of delicacies. There were tacos from El Paso's, sushi fusion hand rolls from Simply Traditional, fish and chips from the Old Anchor, halloumi fries from Eureka, dumplings from the Golden Egg, a small margarita pizza from Romeo's, a veggie curry from Bombay, and my personal favourite, a whole bucket of fried chicken from Uncle Sam's.

We took our meagre amount of food to the side of the river. For hours we sat making our way through the global feast and talking about anything that we could think of: food, desired travel destinations, London's best buildings, and family and friends. I made it my personal mission to eat a bit of everything, and of course, to finish off anything Tomi would let me, using the excuse that otherwise it would go to waste.

I was surprised by how talkative, charismatic, and funny he was, which was different to the version of him I saw at work. The way he talked about his young nieces was somehow both enduring and sweet while leaving me aching at the sides. He then told me about the time he went cliff diving in Morocco during the lads' trip they took every year. Throughout the night, it became more clear that this man was caring, explorative, inquisitive, and daring. Around 22:00 I found myself kissing him along the Thames while the empty bottles and litter floated by on their way to the sea.

We ended the night soon after that as Tomi had a big meeting in the morning. He dropped me off at eleven. Butterflies, steamy windows, and half an hour later, I found myself alone, falling asleep to the idea of another goodnight kiss in his car. Could I have invited him in? Yes, but that would have been unprofessional.

Get the Wine

23:53 Em: Damn it…it was always going to be him...wasn't it?

The walk into work the following morning had me feeling a particular mixture of excitement and nerves that I had only felt once before, when I had kissed the captain of the schools' football team who wanted to keep our budding, but ultimately fake relationship a secret. I was trying to remember Riley's words about how I was single and I had nothing to feel guilty about, regardless of the fact that we all worked together. But, hey, according to the magazine article I read earlier, boys don't talk about this kind of stuff, so I was going to be fine.

My day started well. As soon as I put my bag down, Felix walked into my office with a big mug of coffee.

"Morning, I know you were working late last night, so I thought I would bring you your coffee," he said, putting my favourite yellow mug down in front of me.

"Oh yeah, thank you," I said in a sleepy haze. "It was definitely a late night."

Hey, I wasn't lying, I was technically working – you know, networking.

We chatted for a bit before he left. When I finished the coffee, I took the huge yellow mug back to the kitchenette, washed it, and went back to my office to focus on work.

*Knock Knock

I looked up.

"Good Morning," Tomi said, holding the same yellow mug full of coffee that I had just washed up. "Since it was my fault that you were out late last night, I figured it was my duty to bring you your morning coffee."

"Oh, no it's fine. I had a great time. I am going to need this," I said, a little too enthusiastically, as I reached for the mug to put it on its still-warm coaster. He probably wouldn't be there for that long, so I figured I could just leave it on my desk and 'wait for it to cool down' before I 'drank' it. As I have learned from previous experiences, I don't work well when I have the too-much-caffeine-shakes.

"So, when are we going on our next date?" he asked as he pushed the chair reserved for my clients towards the desk.

Damn it.

"When were you thinking?" I asked with a coy smile while I eyed this second cup of coffee.

"How about Sunday? I know it's a school night, but I promise to have you back earlier than last night."

"It's a date."

"Awesome."

And for the next twenty minutes, he continued to sit in my office and talk about financing my next project.

Needless to say, my hands were shaking when he left and only partially because of the caffeine.

The rest of the morning I felt like a cross between a spoiled princess and a Russian spy. On the one hand, I had two handsome men randomly stopping by with small gifts of chocolate and paperclips, while on the other hand, I constantly had to keep an eye on the door just in case the other came through. Then I had to find an excuse to get rid of whichever one I was talking to. By lunch time, I was exhausted.

*Ding

15:15 Tomi: Hey Em, I was so excited to get to know you. I thought we had such great chemistry and I had a good time last night. I was truly thankful for a chance to get to know you. That is why it was hard to hear that you were out with another man from this office this week. I don't play games and I definitely don't want to be part of your games. Let's stay civil at work but I don't want to see you after this. All the best. Tomi

Shit.

Big. Shit.

Around a quarter to four, I had excused myself from Felix's fifth 'meeting' with me. Between juggling the two different men and my actual work, I hadn't had a moment to myself the entire day. Sitting there on the toilet, Tomi's text hit me like a wall of bricks.

I immediately called Riley for an emergency consultation.

"Girl calm down, you just need to talk to him," was her only advice.

The rest of the work day passed by in moments of agitation and angst as I waited for the clock to strike 17:30.

15:53 Em: Please, no, can we please talk about it
16:19 Tomi: No.
16:20 Em: Please, let me just explain.
16:43 Em: Fine. I'll just wait for you by your car
16:45 Tomi: You don't know when I leave.
16:46 Em: I guess it is going to be a long night.

By 17:35 I was standing next to what I thought was his car. By 17:45 the rest of the car park had emptied. At 18:01, a security guard asked if he could help me with anything, looking at me strangely as I had decided to sit down on the ground. I said no, again, and went back to watching the front of the car park.

18:03 Em: Felix, you shouldn't have told everyone about our date. That was wrong of you. We won't be going on a second one.

At 18:24, my phone battery was at 31%. At 18:46 I messaged Tomi, again no reply. At 19:02 I was starting to get hungry. But there was no way I was going to give up.

"You can't be serious."

I looked up. It was 19:14 and Tomi had stopped a few paces away from me. He was looking both pleased and aghast that I was by his car.

"I told you I was prepared to stay here all night."

"Em, you know that isn't my car right?" I looked at him. I didn't care whose car it was; the only thing that mattered was that he was here. I got up from the floor.

"Come on. My car is over here," he said. "Let's go somewhere else and talk."

We got into his actual car and drove away from the carpark. Tomi was staring at the road. I looked at him trying to think of the best way to start this conversation. Feeling my heart beating faster and faster, I tried to glance at his stern and unforgiving face. I hadn't really thought through what I would say- I'd only planned the waiting part. We drove a few blocks in silence until Tomi parked his car at an abandoned carpark, turned off the radio and looked at me, expectantly. I took a deep breath. *Okay here we go.*

"Thank you for giving me a chance to speak with you. I just needed to say that I am sorry for how I treated you. It wasn't my intention at all to make you feel played." I looked up at him. Tomi remained silent, waiting for me to continue. "To be honest, I'd agreed to go on a date with the other person before you and I had started talking. I didn't plan on this.

I looked back to try and gage his emotional response. Tomi looked at me with an unreadable expression on his face which only caused my nervousness to blossom.

"In hindsight, I could have cancelled, but, well," I took a steadying breath, "it is too late for that now. I didn't want to miss the chance with you so I messaged you back as soon as possible. I had liked you from the beginning and wanted to get to know you but I didn't even know your name. How was I supposed to find you? The other guy and I became friendly, and he asked me out. But then you walked back in and everything changed."

His expression had begun to soften but he kept staring at me so I just kept babbling, "Maybe I should have waited and cleared things with the other one, but I didn't want to wait. I'd been waiting to get to know you since I saw you in the office in my fir...."

I couldn't finish my sentence as Tomi leaned across and kissed me. From that moment on it was Tomi and Tomi only.

The weeks passed, turning March into April. One Wednesday the girls and I were walking by Buckingham Palace as part of our new kick to get fit. Accordingly, we had swapped our weekly dinner for a weekly walk which almost always ended up at our favourite pub. But, you know, the effort was there.

"Em, how did your blood test go at the hospital? I'm so sorry I couldn't go with you," Riley said to me while the others were a few meters ahead.

"It's fine," I replied playing with my bracelets, "Tomi ended up coming with me."

"Really?" she asked, seeming genuinely surprised.

"Yeah. It was so sweet because he remembered what I said about needles scaring me." I added hurriedly, "I mean, I told him he didn't have to. I didn't need him there, but he insisted."

"Wow, that's incredible. Especially since you guys have only been dating, what two months?"

"Yeah, two and a half really. He's just so great like that," I said as Jess opened the door at the pub. "I think this might be something serious."

"It definitely is for him, Em," Riley said. "Be careful with his heart. Anyway, anyone want drinks?"

"Yes. I need one after that tiring walk," Chanel chimed in.

The following months saw Tomi and I make our relationship exclusive. We strived to keep it professional at work but sometimes it was hard when he rocked up in the blue suit with the trousers that highlighted his incredibly round…kneecaps. But we were doing alright in the office and really well outside of work.

In May he bought me an umbrella because someone (him) had stolen it. He wrapped the new one up in a beautiful box and gave it to me as a May Day present.

One early morning in late July he messaged me to pack my bags for a surprise weekend away in Somerset. The hotel he'd booked had three pools (indoor and out), a hot tub on the hotel room balcony and a lovely countryside to frolic in. We indulged in every spa treatment they offered and took many romantic walks in the fields. Proving how well he knew me, Tomi made sure that I always had a glass of champagne in my hand. It was a magical weekend that fulfilled nearly every aspect of my dream. The only thing to have made it perfect was if Idris Elba had walked in.

In August, he had booked a summer holiday weekend away which had to be cancelled because of a work commitment. However he promised to make it up to me. This only ended up being a day trip to Bath but it was still nice. When we were driving home, he let me pick the music on his Spotify.

In September, we signed up for a series of weekly cooking classes on Tuesday nights. The two weekends before Halloween, to mirror our first date, he took me to a Dia de los Muertos event in Camden Market.

By November I'd told him I loved him.

17 December

19:22 Em: Thank you so much for my Christmas presents!
The umbrella keychain is perfect for all of my many keys and
the perfume is divine. Also, you should know that the cheese
is almost gone.
20:19 Tomi: Hahaha I'm sorry we couldn't spend Christmas
together. But after Christmas we can go to that all you can eat
cheese restaurant I told you about.
20:25 Em: I love you
21:01 Tomi: :)

Tomi was great. He respected my space, gave me time
to be with my girlfriends. I loved how much he enjoyed
surprising me. Originally, these surprises had started because he
knew I didn't like not knowing things, so he would tease me
about all these wonderful plans he had for our dates and then
leave to go set them up right then and there. He always had
such a big smile on his face as he went out the door, and down
the street, so I couldn't follow him and "ruin the surprise." It
worked, I always loved what we did, and I grew to love those
moments he was outside making reservations. It became one of
my favourite rituals.

Then, sometime after Christmas, things started to
change between us.

07:31 Em: Missed call
13:13 Em: Missed call
23:45 Tomi: Hey, sorry it's so late and that I missed your
calls. Things with the PhorMula project are getting
complicated. Something about taxes. It's hard to explain. I'll
speak to you tomorrow.

For weeks the group chat looked something like this.

Get the Wine

16:28 Em: *screenshot of Tomi conversation
16:28 Em: This is getting frustrating.
16:28 Em: I haven't talked to him properly in weeks.
16:28 Em: Every time he promises to meet up or to talk with me on the phone he cancels last minute and then apologises for it later.
16:28 Em I know things are busy at work but he has also just said he is going to be spending a lot of time in Brighton because his mom is in and out of hospital.
16:33 Jess: That's not good, babe.
16:33 Jess: You can't build a solid relationship without communication. Even if one of you is going through a hard time. It isn't an excuse.
16:45 Riley: Don't let him ignore you like that. I know he has a lot on his plate. But that isn't how you treat your girlfriend.
16:52 Chanel: If he is having a hard time, you might need to just see how things play out.
16:53 Chanel: Even though it's hard for him right now, you deserve better
17:01 Em: I know. Thanks guys <3

After two months of lack of effort on his part, I knew it was time to let him go. Whenever I tried to talk about this change in communication, he would apologise and things would be better for two days, but it quickly became obvious that it wasn't a good time for him to have a girlfriend.

One day, after nearly a year, I ended things with Tomi. Obviously, Tomi was upset, but I think part of him was relieved.

Aside from wanting to ugly cry every time I saw him at work, we were able to retain a professional and amicable relationship in the office. However, within three months, I was relieved of my continual suffering when he was transferred to a different office in East London for a new project.

Get the Wine

12:48 Em: Girls, I don't know how to do this. It just hurts.
14:02 Riley: Only way to get over someone is to get under someone
15:19 Riley: OR eat the whole cake in the fridge.
15:26 Chanel: You gotta go dancing. We can go during the week!
16:20 Em: I don't think I can do this
16:28 Jess: Girl, get the wine. I'll meet you on the couch in 10 min. I'm on my way

***

***

Sometimes a story isn't finished even when you think it is done…

***

XIII

Jack

Wine Pairing: Il Papavero Rosé Prosecco Brut 2019

***

Regardless of what the magazines say, every woman knows there is such a thing as being too much of a chivalrous gentleman, and those who don't, have never been on a date with Jack.

Jack.

Perhaps he was on a personal mission to redeem all Jacks from the tarnished reputation of the most famous of all the Jacks; or maybe he was simply a true gentleman. Well, if you grew up in Chelsea and owned a flat in Knightsbridge, you had to be a true posh gentleman. There was no way around it.

Jack.

He was the kind of son that any father would proudly introduce to the friendly girl in the neighbourhood and exactly the kind of man you do not want to be introduced to while doing the walk of shame home, with McDonalds in one hand and heels in the other, on a bright Saturday morning.

"Hi Em." called Mr. Vos, my kindly and sweet neighbour from around the corner, stopping me on such a Saturday morning. "I'm so glad we ran into you." Turning to me he gestured to the younger man next to him, "This is my brilliant son Jack, the one I've been telling you about. Jack, this is Em." Turning back to the young man he said, half-joking, half-serious, "Don't mess this up." He laughed and slapped Jack on the shoulder

"Father!" said Jack, in a well-educated voice.

"Jack… Hi, I've heard so much about you. Please excuse me for being such a mess," I said as I tried to fix my untidy hair and straighten the leather jacket draped around my shoulders. "The girls and I just went for brunch … My heel broke…"

He looks down at my shoeless feet and brand new heels.

"McDonalds is an interesting brunch choice," he said blithely.

Damn.

I laughed nervously.

"Oh this is for my roommate," I said out loud.

"I thought you lived alone," chimed in the ever-so-kind and observant Mr. Vos.

"I meant my friend, Riley. She's staying with me for the weekend," I stammered, trying to quickly cover my white lie. "Well, I had better go make sure she's okay. I hope I see you around." I gave an awkward wave with my fully intact heels in my left hand and practically sprinted barefoot down the street into my flat and straight into the washroom to wipe off last night's makeup.

One cheeseburger, box of nuggets, large fries, and long shower later, I was beginning to feel more human. After I had completed my damage check and messaged the girls to say I was feeling atrocious, I had time to reflect on the morning's interaction and decide that it had just never happened. Meeting my silver fox of a neighbour's cute young cub. *No, I don't know who you're talking about. I just moved here. I don't speak English.* Yeah, he was cute but there was no bouncing back from being caught in so many traps. He may have been the fox's son, but he had definitely caught me.

Cringing, I drank my coffee.

A few months passed by without any sign of Vos Jr. I would have forgotten about him except every time I saw Mr.

Vos on the street, I turned bright red and stumbled awkwardly through the interaction.

Get the Wine

11:27 Riley: It's the one year anniversary since she-who-must-not-be-named broke my heart. We're going out. I need to be drunk and make out with some hot strangers tonight.

11:33 Em: aye aye Captain! What's our theme?

11:33 Chanel: YES! I NEED TO DANCE.

11:45 Jess: I can't come into school hungover again. The head of my department keeps making jokes. But, I can come for a bit beforehand!

11:46 Riley: BOOOO but fineee. Teach those kids!

11:55 Em: Aw fine. The rest of you, meet at mine!

They were at my house that Thursday by 19:30. By 21:15 Jess filmed us as Chanel was trying to teach us some Caribbean dance hall steps but we kept turning the wrong way which we definitely blamed on the shots of tequila and not our inability to dance. By 22:43 we were dressed and ready to go and Jess gave us the last warning before she called the Uber from Riley's phone. At 23:23, once Jess had already left, we were actually ready to go and were out standing on the curb sharing a bottle of rosé before the car got there. The bottle had just come back to me when a "Hi Em." came from behind me.

I choked on the wine. There he was. Again. Standing there with a look of acute amusement on his face. *Damn.*

I quickly passed the bottle to Riley and turned around. He had clearly just come from his parents' house wearing a respectable outfit of light jeans and an earthy brown jumper. He had also just clearly ordered an Uber with the phone in his hand.

"Hi," I said awkwardly, trying not to slur my words. "Jack, right? Yeah, Okay. Um...yeah, we aren't...it's...um...we're celebrating tonight!" I threw my hands in the air in a ridiculous fashion.

"I can see," he said with a mischievous look in his eye. "What are you guys celebrating?"

"Singledom!" yelled Riley.

"My Birthday!" yelled Chanel at the same time.

"Her birthday!" I yelled pointing at Riley amidst the chaos.

"I'M EVERY WOMAN! IT'S ONLY MEEEEE!!" burst out singing Chanel at the top of her lungs, wine bottle and hands high in the air, waving to the car full of lads driving past.

"Well happy birthday to…." he laughed, looking from Riley to Chanel and then around at our drunken mess of a group. "Anyway…have fun tonight! Enjoy all the free drinks." He turned back to the street.

We proceeded to stand awkwardly next to each other.

"Em. He's Jack. Like, your Jack the fox, right?" Riley marched up to him and stood having a staring contest with his profile.

"What?" he asked, confused and a tiny bit shocked at this random drunk girl being so close to him.

"It's this Jack, huh?" she said bluntly, turning back to me.

"Ignore her," I said with a red face that matched my jumpsuit.

"Jack! Yeah!" Riley said as I tried to drag her away. "You. Cutie! Give me your phone."

"Where is your phone?" he asked confusedly.

"I just need to call Heaven to let them know we're coming," said Riley. "We're on the lisssst."

"What about the one in your hand?" he said pointing.

"NAWWW I NEED YOUR PHONE. IT'S BETTER!" said Riley with the kind of force only a confident drunk girl can give off.

"Okay," he said somewhere between amusement and annoyance. "But my Uber is only five minutes away. Just make it quick."

Riley grabbed his phone and walked a few paces away.

"I'm so sorry," I turned to him. "She looks quick, but I swear she isn't. Besides, I know where she lives. I can get it back for you."

"Oh no. It's fine. It's funny, really," he said while keeping an eye on Riley.

As our car pulled up, Riley handed Jack back his phone.

"Goodbye Jack the Fox," she said, enunciating his name. "We'll see each other someday."

"Nice to meet you."

"I'm so sorry," I whispered again as I got into the Uber.

"Em! Em! Em! Guess who's getting a text from the cute guy later…IT'S NOT MEEE."

I looked at her horrified.

"YES! You're welcome," she sang as Ari's song about rings and pearl strings came on the radio and we sang loudly into the night.

Don't feel too bad for the driver, he got his revenge on us with the ratings.

For the rest of the night, Chanel and I focused on dancing while Riley focused on Gina, her new dance partner, up in the lounge. A successful night for all of us.

As was our rule, the next day we all got up and, with the power and grace that only coffee can give, made it through Friday.

---

*Ring Unknown number

It was five and I was lying on the couch with my lunch of ice cream and paracetamol. *Oh God, please don't be the heating company. Do I just let it go to voicemail? No, be an adult. I'm old enough to answer the phone without Googling it first. Come on, Em.*

I answered. "Hello?"

"Good evening. Is this Em Mahogany?" asked the familiar voice of embarrassing nightmares.

"Yes. It is. Can I help you with something?" I said, closing my eyes and praying I was wrong.

"It's Jack...you know, the fox. Haha," he laughed while I winced at the memory and hangover induced pain. "How are you feeling? Did you make it to work this morning?"

"It's a work day," I said bluntly but hopefully nicely, "of course I went to work."

"Impressive," he said, not sounding fully impressed. "I was honestly not expecting that to be the answer."

"I'm an impressive person," I said burying my nose in my nearly-done pint of cookie dough ice cream.

"Yes, yes you are," he agreed poshly. I waited for him to continue. "My father speaks very highly of you. I was wondering, would you like to go on a lovely date? I was thinking Saturday if you don't have another brunch planned."

I face-palmed.

"No. I don't have any plans for Saturday," I said through my hands. "That would be nice. What time works for you?"

"Sometime in the afternoon," he stated, "I can pick you up from yours and we can go around there somewhere."

"Great. See you tomorrow. Bye."

"I'll see you tomorrow, Em."

I wasn't sure what I would die of first: mortification or a sugar overdose.

The rain continued to fall for the rest of the evening and well into the early hours of the morning. When we awoke, the gutter outside had been transformed into the Thames. The change in topography of our neighbourhood challenged my go-to date outfit. Flats would be risky, but my wellies just looked a bit ridiculous with my tiny summer dress.

In the end, I kept my flirty dress and decided to gamble with the flats. The sun was breaking through the dark clouds so, by the afternoon, the puddles would surely be gone in time for our date.

At 11:11, I was standing outside my flat with a military jacket in my arms waiting for Jack Vos to arrive. We had agreed to meet at 11:15 but I figured I had no excuse to be late and, since he had seen me at my worst twice, I needed to make a good impression this time. While I was waiting, I saw Mr Vos' car pull out of his driveway and head in my direction. I was watching it drive by so that I could wave as he passed, only to be surprised when he pulled up alongside me. From the opposite side of the car, Jack got out and rushed to my side with an unnecessary open umbrella.

"M'lady," he said, leading me to the car and opening the back door for me.

"Thank you," I said amused. "It is so nice of your dad to lend you the car."

"Hi, Em," I heard from the driver's seat. I spun my head from Jack to the front.

"Mr Vos! Hi?" I said, massaging my neck from the whiplash.

"I'll be your driver for the day," he said courteously.

"The ...the day?" I stammered.

"Well, just to the museum. Diana, Mrs. Vos, and I have some shopping we need to do," he said looking at the empty seat next to him.

"Oh. Okay. Thank you," I said, trying to sound more enthusiastic than I actually felt.

Jack sat in the back with me which, if you didn't think about it too hard, was less awkward than if he had sat up front with his father.

"Em, would you like some water?" Jack asked politely.

"Yes, please," I responded so that I had something to do with my hands when I started to feel the awkwardness.

"Still or sparkling?"

Twenty minutes later, we pulled up outside of the Tate Museum. Jack nearly sprinted to my car door so that I didn't even have a moment to think about opening my own door. He had already paid for our tickets to the special exhibit so he ushered me inside, guiding me with his hand on the small of my back. I felt like a 1960s housewife.

We spent three hours in the museum, going from exhibit to exhibit, marvelling at the talent and skill of the artists on display. It seemed that Jack had a passion for art, or he had simply memorised the life story of every artist in the multiple exhibits we went to. He spent two hours and forty-five minutes lecturing me about every piece we stopped in front of. The other fifteen minutes he talked about the roof tiles after I had made a joke about stealing a picture and sneaking it out through the ceiling.

After a full course in modern art, I needed a coffee. We headed to the local coffee shop around the corner on a quiet street. It wasn't a fancy establishment or even as chic as Chanel's café, but it had coffee. He must have sensed how weak I was feeling because he once again sprinted to open the door for me. He then proceeded to pull out a chair for me after he insisted on ordering for me. While we waited, we had a good conversation about our lives, his childhood, and gossiped a bit about the neighbours who had been on our street since he had been a tod.

"So what is it with the guy in number 82? Every time I walk by he's naked in front of the window. Like, do as you want in your own home, but it's just...I can't see your living room set up when your bare chest is staring out at me."

Jack laughed at my joke.

"He has always been like that. Before he returned home, his mother used to keep the windows shut tight. Maybe, now that she has vacated the premises it makes sense, from a psychological point of view, that he could be rewriting his childhood," he suggested seriously while his eyes got lost in a pleasant memory. He gave me a little smile as he returned to the present moment.

"He was always a bit eccentric, even when we were children." He chuckled. "Oh dear, the stories I have."

I leaned forward.

"Do tell."

Half an hour after my coffee had arrived, I excused myself to go to the ladies. Like the gentleman he was, he stood up to pull out my chair. It was nice to feel appreciated, but I thought it was a bit strange that, when I came back, he was still standing there waiting to push my chair in for me. On a scale of gentleman to Jack, he was just being gentlemanly.

We spent another hour in the cafe getting to know each other. We had been so engrossed in our conversation that we hadn't noticed that it had rained a little while we were inside. When it was time to leave, the car we had called had pulled up across the quiet street from us.

Blocking our way to the car was a puddle. The puddle in question was neither particularly noticeable nor something I would have necessarily thought twice about going around. To be honest, I hadn't even noticed that there was a puddle until Jack raced ahead of me, took off his suit jacket and laid it over said puddle.

Stopping in my tracks, I gave him a look of pure shock. *You can't be serious?*

"I don't want your feet to get wet," he said one hundred percent seriously.

"No, I am not going to step on your jacket," I said as I stared at his beautiful suit jacket that had now shrunk the puddle to nearly half its already small size.

"No, you're going to get your feet wet and then you are going to become cold, and then you're going to get sick," he retorted, seeming to forget that the car was two seconds away from us.

"Honestly, Jack…" I protested, watching his jacket soak up the last bits of the puddle.

"M'lady," he offered as he took my hand and guided me over what once had been a puddle but was now just a soggy jacket lying on the ground.

Well… this will be an interesting story for never have I ever. I stepped onto his jacket and felt the water squirt into my shoe.

Once I was safely across, he pulled out a mysterious plastic bag from his trouser pocket, picked up his jacket, folded it nicely, and put it in the bag.

The entire car ride home he sat with his jacket bag in his lap.

+

That Wednesday, I told the story to the girls. As I told them about the jacket, they snorted into their wine glasses. Riley was laughing so hard she was red in the face and looked like her sides might burst which made our waitress very concerned.

"Why did you do it?" Riley asked, gasping as I grabbed a chip.

"I felt like I had to. It would have been rude not to!"

+

A few days later I called Jack to end things.

17:35

"Good Evening Em."

"Jack, hi. How are you? Listen I had such a great time with you, you are sweet and such an amazing gentleman, but I didn't feel the connection. I know that you will make some girl very happy but I'm not the right one for you. I hope you understand that and we can stay as neighbour-friends?"

"Yes, I would like that very much. I have to agree. While you are very fun, we are not compatible on a dating level. But, it is fun to gossip about the neighbours with you. I think we should keep doing that."

"Haha yes, we should."

"Good! Now to come up with an excuse for my father..."

"Yes, please be gentle with him. Don't want to break his heart."

***

***

Not everyone can be like King Arthur and his Knights of the Round Table.

***

XIV
You Are Not A Bag Of Chips

Wine pairing - Expensive but disappointing champagne

***

"Do we have to watch this movie?" Riley begged as we put on the film.

"Yes, we do. You lost fair and square, so we get to choose!" I said as the opening notes to *Mamma Mia 2* sounded over the speakers.

"But...but…"

"Oh shush, you made us watch a gruesome murder documentary and we didn't complain. So just shut up, drink the wine and enjoy your free Abba concert," Chanel joked as she handed Riley her nearly empty wine glass for a refill.

"At least this way, we can all sleep in our own beds tonight," I added.

Riley sighed.

Chanel and Jess laughed and broke out in an off-pitch rendition of *I Kissed the Teacher*.

We settled into the movie, if you can call getting up and dancing every fifteen minutes 'settling down.' Riley assumed her usual role as our butler during these musical masterpieces and refilled our bottomless wine glasses and always-empty food platter while we jumped and sang to every song that came on. None of us really understood her strong dislike for musicals because she was usually the first one out on the dancefloor and the last to leave in a club. She just really didn't like Abba; one negative of having Riley as one of your best friends. Well, a neutral really because of the whole butler act.

*Ding

"Riley, can you get my phone? I'm in the middle of my performance. This is my favourite part of the movie!"

I sang to the beat of *Angel Eyes*.

"Oh my god, Em, you should look at this DM slide..."

"The DM sliders can wait," I sang dramatically as I continued to dance standing on my chair.

"No, seriously, this one has a blue tick."

We paused the movie. There was a moment of silence before we all started talking over each other.

"What?"

"Who is it?"

"Do we know him?"

"Is it some influencer?"

"No. Everyone knows him!" Riley said in seriousness.

"Come on! Who is he?" I asked.

"You know that guy who sings that one song you were listening to yesterday..." Riley hinted as she showed me the screen.

"OH, him?" I got off the chair and drew closer to look at the phone.

"I can't wait to come to your LA wedding!" Chanel yelled.

"OR," Jess interjected excitedly, "Get married at Aunty Carol's Wedding Venue."

"Don't forget us when you're rich and famous!"

"Why is he messaging me?" I asked, confused. "Is it from my work Instagram?"

"No," Riley responded, passing the phone to me and flicking her long brown hair away. "However, he is asking you to come to a 'meeting' in a hotel…."

"What?"

I reread it out loud.

21:39
Yeahlikeweregoingtotellyouwhoitis: Hey gorgeous. Such an elegant lady. I'm in London right now... in Central. Wanna hangout tonight?

I paused while I thought of a clever response in my holey ex boyfriend's hoodie that covered my boyfriend-style faded pajama shorts.

21:51
EmEmEm: Sorry, I have a previous engagement with the girls. Have a good one.

We put the phone on the table and resumed the movie. However, none of us were getting up to sing anymore. All of us were sat there waiting for something to happen next. Still playing butler, Riley went to the kitchen to get more wine.

*Ding
We all scrambled to the phone.

"Who is it?" Riley shouted from the kitchen.
"It's freakin' Josh….Not! Now! Josh!" I yelled, frustrated. I put the phone back on the table.

Five minutes passed by with Cher singing Jess' favourite song, *Fernando,* in the background.

"Are we certain it sent?" Jess said, mid-song. Even Jess, our ultimate musical fan, couldn't focus. This was serious.
"Yeah, the Wi-Fi in here is really bad," Chanel added.
"You should double check, Em," Riley said.

I picked up my phone. They gathered around as I opened up my messages.

"He unsent the message!" Jess exclaimed.

"Did you get a screenshot at least?" asked Chanel.

"NO!" I cried. "I was too surprised."

"Well, there goes your magic red carpet, Em," Riley said.

"It's fine," I replied, putting my phone down, annoyed that we didn't think to get a screenshot. How often do you get a message from an A-list celebrity?-

"Jess…"

"I don't know everyone in Hollywood!"

Chanel sighed.

"Ugh, think of the fancy things you could have done."

Chanel, Riley, and I spent the rest of the night contemplating our dreamy, glittery, sunny Hollywood life.

The next morning, I returned back to my rainy London life where I was brutally reminded that I couldn't just skip the queue for coffee and still had to take the Circle line to work because Alfie (our sexy driver) didn't exist.

I was sitting in my overcrowded and messy office looking out over the grey skyline wishing for just one second that I could be in LA on this foggy Spring day. Just as I was trying to make myself feel better by repeatedly thinking about how lucky I was to be living in the greatest city in the world, it started to rain for the seventh time that day.

During my breaktimes, I looked for cheap flights to California.

On my way home, I checked my social media; three notifications from Instagram and one from Josh, again.

Not. Now. Josh! I thought to myself as I anxiously opened up Instagram messages.

17:19
Yeahlikewe'regoingtotellyouwhoitis:
*one unopened photo
*unsent
"Add me on Snapchat...userFaFrY27963"

I would have stopped in my tracks if I wasn't already on the escalator going down the tube.

Open! Open! I prayed frantically pressing on the icon.
*no internet connection
Damn you underground, no service! I spent the next twenty minutes playing out every scenario in my head about what the unsent photo could have been.

Once on the train, the internal war raging inside me drowned out the screeching of the tracks. *This guy was way too out of my league to be serious. He was way famous. He filled stadiums. How did he even find me? What does he want from me...okay, we all know what he wants from me...he asked for my Snapchat. But should I respond? Do I entertain the idea? Is this moving all too fast? But, I would look so good in a black dress on the red carpet...Oh what about with gold shoes?* The rest of the ride I spent dreaming about my debut in Hollywood on his arm.

Once above ground and safely on the correct bus (having almost gotten run over because I realised I was on the wrong side of the street) I once again debated whether to add him on snapchat or not. I looked through his profile again. It seemed legit, I reasoned with myself, plus, there was a blue tick. *Instagram doesn't just give those out to anyone.*

Initiating my inner detective in a way that would have made Jess proud, I found his other social media links attached to his Instagram, They all were verified and none of them mentioned anything about hacking. His most recent posts were from London.

It did seem pretty legit.

When I got home, I Facetimed Chanel, who was the most mature of us.

"Let the wine decide," was her sage advice.

While on the phone, I looked for something to drink. As I hadn't gone on my weekly shop so there was only one drink in the flat: cheap champagne which had been sitting on my shelf since my birthday more than a few years before. I poured myself a glass and took a sip. A bit flat, but whatever, it had alcohol in it.

"Yep," I proclaimed after I downed my flat bubbly. "I'm adding him."
"GOOD GIRL!" Chanel cried out. "Even if it goes nowhere, this will make a great story."
"Alright," I said slowly. "I added him. I'm going to put you on pause for a minute so I can send him a snap."
"Okay."
"Done. Sent. Now, let's see…oh my god that was fast."
"What?" Chanel demanded. "Has he opened it already?"
"No," I replied in shock. "He's replied."
"Oh damn. Okay, go check it out, I'll be right here..." Chanel encouraged.
"It most definitely is him," I announced after a second, "but he seems to have lost his shirt."
"Girlllll SHOW ME."

"I can't screenshot because it will notify him," I said a bit frantically but with excitement.

"Don't you have your old phone still?"

This was one of the many benefits of having Chanel as one of your best friends. She was always thinking outside the box.

He and I Snapchatted for half an hour while I used my second phone to record everything. It wasn't like I was going to sell the photos or videos, I just needed proof that this was actually happening.

I mean, he was famous. I was broke. That wasn't a legal battle I was prepared to chance.

The next morning, I woke up to five Snapchats. Three of which I can't talk about here (like seriously, why do some guys think we want to see that) and two of which were wondering when he was going to see me next.

19:00

Em365: Next? We haven't even met yet.

userFaFrY27963: come on babyy

Em365: I still haven't even hear you speak

Em365: For all I know, you could be a catfish who wants to take me to a buffet.

userFaFrY27963: uve seen me babe

Em365: Pictures don't prove anything.

userFaFrY27963: so how can i prove to you who i am? have you googled me?

Em365: Just video call me so I can have a conversation with you

---

My phone started ringing with a Snapchat call.

I nearly dropped my phone in sheer panic as the phone kept vibrating in my hand. I ran to the laundry room (what? It had the best lighting) and answered the call.

"Wow, I didn't think you'd call right away," I said, trying to sound cool and confident while really freaking out on the inside. It's a bizarre feeling talking to someone you've seen on TV playing in massive stadiums on your tiny phone screen.

"Of course I would, Em," he replied casually. "I wanna meet you. I am who I say I am."

In the background, I heard someone calling him. His brown eyes flicked back to me as he said hurriedly into the phone, "I want to take you on a proper date. I'm leaving in two days. Come to my hotel tonight. I'll send the car." Before I could reply he hung up.

After another medicinal glass of flat champagne and several chocolates, I sat down and thought about this seriously. It could be fun. It would definitely be a story. But what was it going to cost me? A little while later, the rest of the girls were home, so I asked them to get on a group Facetime call.

The girls talked while I listened.

"Should she go?" Jess questioned.

"No, I think it's a bad idea," Chanel weighed in.

"What? It's a great idea!" Riley objected, "Every time he comes on the radio, she can tell people she went on a date with him."

"A date?" Chanel pointed out, "What he is offering isn't a date. It is him ordering her to his room like some kind of dinner that you get off Uber Eats."

"Yeah, but he's famous, he doesn't want to be seen in public with anyone," Riley argued.

"That isn't an excuse," I chimed in. "If you want to see me, you take me on a proper date. No matter who you are. I'm worth a real date."

"Come on! Take one for the team," Riley begged.

"I'm all in if he takes me out," I said. "But I'm not a burger you can order from McDonald's. I'm a steak that is served with a three-course meal and the most expensive bottle of fine wine."

Even Riley clapped for that little speech.

Right as I hung up with the girls, he sent me another message.

19:22
userFaFrY27963: What's your address, babezz? do u have a little black dress?
Em365: Why? Do you want to borrow it?
userFaFrY27963: nahhh, I want to see it on my bedroom floor tonight
Em365: Sorry, I'm not interested. All the best.

I locked my phone.

Two minutes later he called me.

"Come on babe. What if I take you to LA?" he drawled into the phone.

I took a deep breath and said, "I can't go to LA because I have something called a job that won't pay for me to take time off without any notice."

"I can pay for it. Don't worry. Just come," he begged.

"Sorry," I said definitively. "My mom always told me not to fly halfway around the world with strangers." I hung up.

Oh well, I ruminated, getting ready for bed and quite proud of myself for knowing my worth, *maybe next time he's in town, he'll try again.*

***

***

He does still check my stories and will send me the occasional picture.

I don't usually respond.

Certain stories are better left unread than others.

***

XV
Letter

Wine Pairing: Nope, you need two shots of tequila for this one.

***

It was meant to be a celebratory Friday evening in May. We were supposed to be toasting Chanel's new relationship as well as signing for her second cafe's lease with a few drinks at the pub. For the first time in a while, we were all free on a Friday. But as soon as Riley and I walked in, everything changed. When she heard the door, Chanel turned to look at us.

"Em…Are you okay?"

"What happened?"

"Are you alright?"

"I have a story about Tomi," I said to the girls as Riley looks at me with empathy. "I move to nominate him to become the king of the FNC list."

"Sure, but what happened?"

I pulled out the unopened letter.

++

Earlier that day, I was at home doing some bicep curls with Dorritos and guacamole while waiting for Riley to get to mine. As her phone had developed a bad habit of vibrating for no reason, she needed to stop by the phone store near my flat to get her phone fixed before we all met for dinner. I had just started my intense arm workout and the film *Burlesque* when I heard Riley let herself in. There was a pause before the door shut.

"Em?" Riley walked in with confusion in her brown eyes, her jacket half off and shoes still on, looking down at the top letter of several envelopes in her hand. "What was Tomi's last name?"

"Hendrics," I responded automatically over my shoulder. "Why?" I turned to look at her.

Saying nothing, she handed me the letters. The first letter was addressed to him. While it was my mailing address it clearly had 'Tomi Hendrics' written on it, which was weird as we hadn't talked in over a year. There had been no texts, no calls, no emails from him. Nothing in the way of trying to start again. If this was a letter addressed to me with his name in the sender area, my heart would have stopped. But instead I was confused. He had never used my address for anything other than Uber Eats Delivery; nor had he ever asked to use it.

I turned the envelope around. Scrawled across the front in big blue letters was a well-known bank logo. Through the envelope, I could feel the shape of a thick card and the raised numbers you get on a debit or credit card.

I looked at Riley who was stood in front of me waiting for some kind of explanation.

"Why is he getting junk mail sent to my address? And why are they sending a card? Isn't that dangerous?"

"Who knows," Riley said as confused as I was. "I mean, it is weird but what does it matter? You haven't spoken to him in what, a year?" She shrugged. "I'm going to get ready for my phone appointment. When I get back, we can watch something else before we head out to meet everyone." She headed towards the bedroom to change out of her work clothes into something more comfortable. Ten minutes later, she was gone.

While *Burlesque* was playing in the background, I sat and stared at the envelope for a little while longer. Eventually I pulled out my phone and did what every good girl does: research. The bank website advertised options for buying currency for your travels or a travel card that offered a gold prepaid gift card.

Well, that must be what this letter is, I tried to explain to myself, playing with my bracelets. In the film, Ali and Marcus started their intimate love scene while I reflected on my past relationship with Tomi.

But why is he sending it to me? Isn't that just something he would send to his house? It was such a nice house. He had better taste in interior design than I did. I wish we could have spent more time there, but all the traveling and holidays were nice. I mean that's probably why he got this card. Maybe he was trying to surprise me? But why did it come so late?

Suddenly, on the tele screen, the angry ex barged in on the still-sleeping Ali and Marcus cuddling in bed and proceeded to accuse Ali of sleeping with an engaged man.

Fuck. He's married.

He is *SO* married. SHIT.

Why else would someone use a prepaid card? Why would anyone ever use a prepaid card? Of course- because there are no bank statements to explain.

Fuck. He always paid with a card, never with cash but he always had to stop at the cash machine to withdraw money when we were together.

Fuck. That was why we were rarely at his house. She was there.

Fuck. Those calls outside...those weren't for me. That was her.

Fuck. That was why he never stayed over the whole night. He didn't care about my 'waking up too early,' he had to get home to her.

Fuck. The perfume. Fuck. Every weird timing of our dates and trips. That was why we barely ever went out for dinner. Fuck; that was why, when we did, it was always to darkly-lit restaurants on weeknights. Fuck. They weren't just for the romantic atmosphere. Fuck. It was sent to my house so she would never find out.... FUCK.

Fuck. He probably forgot to cancel. Or he ordered a new one. Oh My God, he has to have a new girlfriend.

Before I knew it, I had my shoes on, my keys in hand, and my jacket somewhere around my elbows as I ran across the street to the phone store. Somehow, I saw Riley through my clouded vision and hazy brain. I ran to her.

"Riley!" I cried out as she simultaneously exclaimed, "Em, is everything okay?"
"He's married."
I couldn't tell which of our faces was the most shocked: mine, hers, or the guy behind the counter.
"WHAT?" they both exclaimed.

I told them the whole story.

++

Back at the restaurant, Jess was already typing away furiously on her phone. Chanel stared at me, her jaws on the ground and her hands over her open mouths. Riley just stroked my shoulder.
"Oh. My. God."
"What?"
"No... Are you sure?"
"Em."
"It could be a mistake."
"Em."
"I can think of a few reasons."
"Em!"
"Maybe it's not what you think?"
"Em." Jess touched me lightly on the arm. I looked up at her knowing eyes. "He's married. Her name is Lucy. They were married for five years before you guys met. Her recent picture is of the two of them in Cyprus a month ago."
Outside, the world stopped for a second as we dissected this information while Jess showed how there was a

new article published on the company website that had a photo of the two of them with both of their names under it. Inside, my heart dropped in my stomach. I felt dizzy and faint.

Chanel came around to give me a hug from behind. Riley went to go get us some shots and chips while the other two gave me time to collect my thoughts as they proclaimed him the king of the FNC. To solidify it, we took the first shot.

"So, what are we going to do?" Jess asked me calmly. "Are we going to confront him? Egg his house? Have you messaged her?"

"I have to message her, huh?" was my blank-faced response.

***

***

Sometimes the ending of the story is as much of a shock to you as it is to her.

Sometimes the ending of a story changes your whole perception of the story.

Sometimes the ending of the story is passed out of your hands and into hers.

***

XVI

His Latest Heartbreak

Wine Pairing: Cloudy Bay Sauvignon Blanc 2020

***

The birds that had woken me up that morning were singing to me now as we walked through Hyde Park for a celebratory late summer picnic. I had cycled home in the heavy morning air, which indicated that it was going to be another sweaty day after a refreshing night camping under the stars and our blankets in Riley's garden. It felt like we'd been teleported to the tropics, and all we wanted to do was be outside.

It was the perfect day with a sky as clear as crystals. The heat of the summer day was dying as the sun hung low in the sky. Around us the bees buzzed from flower to flower, ensuring life would continue for yet another day. We sat in the middle of the field with similarly-minded people on all sides of us munching on supermarket fruit cups and drinking French rosé. Footballs weaved between us as players of all ages chased them with supportive cheers and laughter coming from the sidelines.

I snapped back to the moment as Chanel offered me some more wine.

"We're out of the white. What should we open next?"

We picked the rosé on the right because it looked colder than the other ones. Pouring ourselves our third glass, we continued munching on my decadent veggie platter (which had been battered on the back of my bicycle), Riley's selection of Tesco's Finest crisps, and Jess's salami and brie (which were not looking good in the heat of the day). The only things that had been of any quality were the pastries from Chanel's bakery, which obviously hadn't lasted very long.

"Look at how pretty Riley looks," Jess said, motioning to Riley, who was coming back from the toilet, in her summer dress and hair dancing behind her. She squinted, "Wait. Why does she look so suspicious?"

Chanel and I looked around.

"She does!"

"What did she do?"

"Bets it's a guy," I said, drinking my rosé.

Without warning, Riley started to sprint over to us. As there didn't seem to be anyone nor a football to explain her sudden sense of urgency, we all greeted her with a look of concern. Jess held out a cup of water to her as she approached.

"EM!" Riley said, catching her breath. "Don't look now, but the group of guys behind us, you know, the ones who were having a kick around earlier. The one with the tattoos on his arm, he keeps glancing over at you. I was trying to get his attention as I was going to the toilet, but he was just looking at you! Em, he is so handsome."

As she was speaking, all of the girls took their turn to catch a glimpse at him. There he was reclining on the grass with his sunglasses on laughing with his friends but occasionally looking over at us.

Oh damn.

"Like you look up "handsome" in the dictionary, it would be his picture," Jess agreed, "You have to go talk to him."

I turned around, and assessed the situation.

"Riley," I turned to look at her. "You go. Please! Can you go give him my number? He is so hot, I can't do it," I pleaded with her.

"No. I said at Winter Wonderland that the Silver Fox was going to be last time. I've helped you four times since then but NO! You have to do it."

"Chanel? Plea…" I turned to my last hope.

"No. I came with you to the dentist last week. Woman up and go over there."

They left me no choice.

I took a big sip of wine, stood up, dusted off my blue dress, slipped on my suede sandals, took a deep breath and turned around.

We locked eyes.

Strong jaw line, high cheekbones, a face that was blessed by the gods (aka his parents). Under his white t-shirt peeked out well defined arms that were covered in black and grey tattoos. I was too far away to see what they were but I could tell that his arms were built to carry me. He smiled, and for a second, the sun hid in shame.

I turned around.

"I can't do this," I said, going to sit back down.

"No!" Riley grabbed me by the shoulder. "You. Must. Do. This. Right. Now." She spun me around and gently pushed me off the blanket.

Balancing myself, I looked up at him. He was still smiling at me, almost laughing. He stood up and walked over.

Well, I guess I have no choice now. I took another steadying breath and stumbled towards him.

"Hi," he said with a husky bass voice that rumbled.

"Hi," I squeaked more than said, twisting my bracelet. There was a moment of awkward silence. "Well, bye," I said, waving and going to turn around. The girls signalled me to stay there.

"Ah come on!" he joked as he reached to stop me. "I've walked all the way over here. What's your name?" He smiled encouragingly and I melted.

"I'm Em," I said, extending my hand. "What's your name?"

"Hi, I'm Jamie."

"Jamie...Jamie with the nice football skills."

"Em, Em with the pretty face."

"Oh, this old thing? Thanks, my mamma gave it to me."

"Well, your mother did the world a favour."

Ten minutes later I returned triumphant to the sound of applause from the girls. We poured the bottle of white wine which was the only cold bottle we had left and toasted my new organic match.

Jamie and I texted for two weeks about everything: politics, social issues, latest reads, classic movies, and the weather. It was lovely to have such stimulating conversation with a guy I was interested in. Any time he talked about his work with solar energy, or really anything about the environment, I needed a good ten minutes to research what he was talking about before giving him a response.

We tried to arrange a date but both of our schedules were busy. I had a new campaign that was about to launch and he had a big project due within the month.

++

"Chicken soup and orange juice for the sick!" I said as Chanel opened the door.

"Come in," she said. "Thanks for coming to hang out. I've been so bored." Even when she was in three-day-worn pyjamas and deathly sick, Chanel still looked flawless. "I was just picking a movie, what were you thinking? I've got Crazy Rich Asians, The Greatest Showman, or Mamma Mia?"

"I haven't seen Crazy Rich Asians in a while. Want to do that one?"

"Yeah," she said as she passed me a cuppa. "Tea for you, juice for me, and eye candy for both of us."

Girl Get The Wine

18:00 Em: Jess can you hook us up with Henry Golding or Harry Shum?!!
18:13 Jess: oh shut up. Ask your own Hollywood guy
18:20 Riley: hahahaah

We were halfway through the movie and thoroughly enjoying our eye candy when I got a notification on my phone.

*ding

19:20 Jamie: Good evening Em. This not seeing each other due to work is getting a bit silly now. I have a proposal for you. I have a work function tomorrow night that I am required to attend. How would you like to accompany me to said work function at 18:30 at Shane and Co in Temple. Let me know!

I started to type back when Chanel pointed out the best bit of the movie.
*ding
I looked down.

19:21 Em: Ye
19:32 Jamie: Okay then. I'll send you the address and meet you there.

"Shit!" I said looking up at Chanel. "How do I fix this?" I showed her my half typed accidental response.

"Naw, it's fine. You're going on the date anyway. Don't worry about it."

The next morning, after staring at my wardrobe for so long I was going to be thirty minutes late to work, I decided to go with my first option of a light white jumpsuit, navy blue belt and chunky heels, then opting for a simple gold chain and bangles, with dangly gold earrings with pearls on the end. For work, I wore a blue striped button-up over it to be a bit more work- appropriate, and decided to bring a blue blazer in case it got cold.

At the end of the day, I was able to escape my own Friday after-work drinks and rush to the tube. Fifteen minutes later I was at Temple. I had taken off my work shirt in the office to show off the jumpsuit's flattering top but brought the blazer in case it got chilly.

Unsure of where the actual location was and getting misdirected on maps one too many times, I texted Jamie, only to realise seconds later that I had passed the doors three times. Hurriedly, I walked past the big flashing diamond sign and walked in.

"Can I get your name for the guest list?" the hostess welcomed me.

"I'm actually with someone. His name is Jamie."

"Jamie…" she said, scrolling her finger down the list. "Last name?"

"Um…"

"Em! Beat me to it," he smiled as he walked down the stairs. Greeting me, he gave me a kiss on the cheek, turned to the hostess and confidently said, "She's with me." He grabbed my hand and pulled me past the barrier. My legs were jelly, making it difficult to keep up. As I walked past the hostess winked at me.

The sound of a trumpet floated down the steps as we made our way to the party. Every time the doors opened from somewhere above us, you could hear a loud jazz band playing and the sound of people talking and laughing. When we got inside, we were greeted with the clink of cheering glasses and the sight of well-dressed people enjoying their summer afternoon.

I looked up. On the ceiling was a painted mural meant to replace the summer's day outside with fluffy clouds and cherubs. The walls were decorated with paintings that I had seen copies of in the Art History textbooks I had skimmed in Uni. One side had windows that faced out to the river and doors that led to a balcony.

"Shall we go outside?"
"Yeah, it's so lovely out today. Let's enjoy it."

After getting our drinks and stopping to greet a few dozen people, we finally made our way to the balcony. If I had thought inside was beautiful, it was nothing to the view. Helping to keep the overhead roof high above us were proud columns of white stone connected by a matching small guard with just enough space to sit upon if it wasn't for the ugly metal railing that must have been installed as a safety feature.

From where we were standing, you could look over the rooftops of London. From one side, you could see the river winding its way through the metropolis and tiny ferries slowly drifting over it's secret-filled waters. The sun was at that perfect time of day when the light was turning from daylight to that silky light before golden hour, drenching the grandiose buildings around us with magnificent, dancing shades of light you could almost touch. In the distance, the bells of St. Paul rang out.

"This is beautiful," I gasped in admiration looking out over the city.
"Yeah, but it will take us forever to get drinks," Jamie pointed out, raising his nearly empty glass and laughing.

The date was going well. We were disturbed a few times when his colleagues interrupted our flowing conversation.

Each time he would introduce me to whomever he was talking to. We politely exchanged a few pleasantries with them before returning back to our conversation.

The event was to celebrate the launch of their latest solar panel design that would "increase solar power in the household two-fold and reduce the need for crude energy sources in ten years." Impressive, but no match for the selection of canapés they had.

The sun was setting over the west side of London sinking the city into a hazy golden hue that reflected off the handsome buildings. In the background the jazz band was playing a string of notes that sounded like *The Girl from Ipanema*.

"Jamie? Is that you? Hi. How are you?" a man said, approaching from behind Jamie.

Jamie's face changed to stone as he turned around to greet the man and the two women that were with him.

"Hi Don. How are you? Nice to see you, Maggie. Claire, you, look well," he said, his voice emotionless.

The three of them looked quizzically at me.

"Hi," I choked out, almost spraying them with rosé. "I'm Em." I gave them my brightest smile and reached to shake each of their non-extended hands as they looked at me with a mixture of disgust and surprise.

Don was a balding man in his late sixties with a pleasant face that was weary with the work of the day. On his arm was a majestic older lady in purple with perfectly coiffed hair and a pearl necklace that pulled away from the stern look on her face. Next to her was a beautiful, petite brunette in a stunning little black dress who looked like she wanted to be anywhere else but here.

While Don and Jamie awkwardly conversed I tried to talk to the ladies. As they seemed a bit more reserved, which could have been because of my nearly spitting on them, I tried to find a common interest to introduce a conversation. But when I kept getting responses of "I don't know," or just no response to questions about their favourite travel and food, I gave up. I filled the silence with a story about fishing in Finland before excusing myself to get another glass of wine.

When I returned about twenty minutes later, Don, Maggie, and Claire had left, leaving Jamie standing with his hands on the rails looking out over the city with a sad and pensive look on his face.

"Is everything okay?"

"I didn't think they would be here."

"What? What do you mean? Who?"

He looked out quietly over the slowly darkening city, and then took a deep breath.

"That couple and their daughter; that was my ex-fiancée and her parents."

I nearly dyed my jumpsuit with rosé as the sun set behind the skyline.

"Yep."

"I'm sorry. I didn't realise. Um. Do you want me to leave?" I said, not really sure of what to say.

"No. I just need a moment." He paused, "We only broke up a month ago."

"Oh," I said as I leaned on the rail and joined him looking out over the city as the first star peeped out in the evening sky.

For the rest of the night, I was an awkward tortoise. At least, that's what I felt like. Out of respect for Claire, I didn't want to flirt or show too many physical displays of affection towards Jamie. It seemed like he had the same idea as he started going out of his way to get the people who stopped to say hello to stay for longer than was necessary by asking them a string of unrelated and personal questions. He tried to play it cool, but I noticed him constantly searching around the room for Claire.

At the end of the night, the beautiful first kiss I was hoping to get ended up being a sweet kiss on the cheek as he opened my Uber car's door for me. I spent the ride home looking out the window thinking about Jamie, his ex-fiancée and a past holiday in Rhodes.

A week later I was getting ready for bed when I got my last text from Jamie.

22:03 Jamie: Hi Em. I'm sorry I didn't message you after the function but I realised that I'm just not ready to date anyone yet. You're a great person and I wish you all the best.

Bitch I know.

I answered with a kind response, sent a screenshot of the message to the girls, archived our conversation and continued to brush my teeth.

***

Afterwards

So I've been thinking: why is it that women are called serial daters when they are dating? How did this perception of the single woman come to be?

Women are not supposed to date a lot of people. When a woman has multiple dates in a week she is called nasty names and her value is seen to go down. She is shamed for dating. But then how else are we supposed to find that soulmate if we don't date people? What do you want me to do? Go for the first person who tells me they're interested in me? I don't fucking think so.

I'm a valuable person in and of myself who deserves to find someone who is my equal. Why should I settle?

We are told from our childhood that our purpose is fulfilled once we have found a single person to share our lives with. Books and films sell us on this idea of 'the soulmate'. That one person who is supposed to be your all- your everything. But one person can't fulfill your every need. That is so much to ask of an individual. Only you can be your everything.

Besides, what happens to our friends once we have met that one all-encompassing person? We don't mean for it to happen, but they do just seem to disappear.

Friends are an important part of everyone's life. They are the people who truly know you and love you for everything that you already are with no other expectation than that you will love them as fully as they love you. They will call you out when you need someone to give you that harsh reminder and they will give you the support when you can't give it to yourself. I mean, you can't have a romantic relationship with someone without there being a solid friendship to support it.

Maybe our soulmate isn't just one person. Maybe it's a group of people. Maybe our soulmates are our friends. Honestly, I think the amount of soulmates you can have are numberless.

It is for me.

At the end of the day, my girls are my everything. You can spend an eternity looking for someone, hell you might even find that someone, but your close friends are irreplaceable.

Does that mean I'm going to stop dating since I've found my soulmates already? Hell no! Dating is fun. I like dating. I like meeting new people and gaining new experiences.

So I'm going to keep dating. If I find someone along the way. Great, but it will just be an added bonus to my already full life.

+

A few days ago, a cute guy from one of those dating apps asked to spontaneously meet up after I was stood up by another guy (don't worry, I'll tell you about it later), I had a bit of a mental debate within myself.

"What? Are you really going to go on two dates on the same night? Well, not that the first one even really counted as a date...besides, how is he going to know? But isn't this kind of a quick turnaround?"

"Whatever," I said out loud to myself, "who really cares?"

22:24 Em: Why not!

++

Some might call it serial dating;

I call it single.

***

***

Thank you

To all of our friends who have supported us throughout this writing process. Thank you for your valuable and honest feedback. Thank you for your love and always hyping us up.

Thank you to the various great men who are the inspiration of our stories. They might not be you, but you were still in our thoughts when we created these characters.

To our families and other friends…SURPRISE!

WE WROTE A BOOK :)

Love,

Em and Am

***

Girl Get the Wine

by Em Rina and A.M. Lee

These pages are for you to write down your dating adventures.

Happy dating :)

My FNC List

If you find yourself on this list it is because you have been found to have displayed clown behaviour. As a result, you are a clown. Any persons being found to text anyone on the FNC list will be punished by paying for all drinks at the next dinner.

My Dating Rules

Date 1

Pair this date with:

Date 1

Date 1

Date 2

Pair this date with:

Date 2

Date 2

Date 3

Pair this date with:

Date 3

Date 3

Date 4

Pair this date with:

Date 4

Date 4

Date 5

Pair this date with:

Date 5